"I thought you would be a knight in shining armor," said Devonny. She did not touch her tears, but let them lie on her cheek and throat. "I thought you would save me. Why did you come if you weren't going to save me?"

"It isn't like I meant to come," said Tod.

She looked stricken. As if he had slapped her. Fleetingly, Tod considered what his mother would do to him were he ever to raise a hand to a girl.

He didn't want any heavy thoughts here, or any responsibility. People had to be responsible for themselves. "You don't need saving, Devonny. You just need guts." Tod had no sympathy for weakness. "I'm going," he told her.

She held out her hands, and the flowery bracelet fell from one wrist, and her voice trembled on, saying more, but he stepped back, grabbed the pump handle, closed his eyes—and it worked. Her words followed, crying without sound, *But I need you!*

# Prisoner of Time

### CAROLINE B. COONEY

LAUREL-LEAF
BOOKS

Published by
Bantam Doubleday Dell Books for Young Readers
a division of
Random House, Inc.
1540 Broadway
New York, New York 10036

**Visit us on the Web! www.randomhouse.com**

**Educators and librarians, for a variety of teaching tools, visit us at www.randomhouse.com/teachers**

ISBN: 0-440-22019-X

RL: 6.4

Reprinted by arrangement with Delacorte Press

Printed in the United States of America

September 1999

10  9  8  7  6  5  4  3  2  1

OPM

# Prisoner of Time

# ONE

$\mathcal{D}$evonny Aurelia Victoria Stratton was smuggling a love letter.

It was not a love letter to Devonny, but that was all right. Devonny was not ready to fall in love with an unsuitable man. It was much more fun to help her friend Flossie, who had fallen in love with an unsuitable man.

The folded letter lay inside her glove, hidden by lace and ribbons.

No one must suspect.

If Flossie's father caught the boy who wrote the letter, Mr. Van Stead would throw him into the quarry and smile as he died. This added a certain excitement to every stolen moment.

As for Devonny, her father had been stomping around in a rage lately, throwing things at the servants and beating his horse. He was a heavy man, fond of his whiskey and pipe. Packed into his starched white shirt and closely fitted black jacket, he looked as if bad news would burst him. Devonny would be in trouble if Father discovered her part in Flossie's flirtation.

Devonny intended to fall in love with a man like her father. Well—not mean, dishonest and brutal. Not that part. But like the man who left school in the eighth grade, began by delivering coal, and forty years later was one of America's wealthiest men. Self-made.

Devonny loved that: taking your self and making it. Father had glimpsed Fortune, and then went out and created it.

Devonny, too, would be self-made. A Self-Made Woman. These were new times. And not only that, Devonny had heard about women who had done incredible things. Achievements as important as a man's. Of course she wasn't sure it was true, because she had heard this from a peculiar source—a person who had visited from a future century. Devonny pushed all those memories from her mind. The end of this century was only a few years away. She could see for herself how life was changing. Why, a woman in New York City was writing articles for a newspaper just as if she were a man! Women were opening settlement houses to help the poor. They were marching to get the vote.

Devonny was not interested in journalism, the poor or votes. She wanted to be a woman of business. Sometimes she could not fall asleep at night for thinking about the business she would create.

But in Devonny's circle, a lady's first concern must always be men. Devonny must constantly plan how to make the lives of men more comfortable. She must be an adornment, so men could be proud of her. Luckily she was very beautiful and had very fair skin. Her father continually reminded Devonny that nothing mattered except her complexion and *his* money.

Soon it would be time to tell Father that he was wrong. Something else mattered. She, Devonny Aurelia Victoria Stratton, was going to make a fortune of her own. She smiled happily, thoroughly enjoying the danger and the pleasure of Flossie's forbidden romance. Love letter crisp against her palm, she strolled onto the veranda, pretending leisure and boredom, so that nobody would guess she was on an urgent mission of love.

There sat her father's houseguest, also writing a letter. The moment Lord Winden saw Devonny, he set blotting paper over his paragraphs and rose to his feet, bowing to her.

Devonny could not help herself. Knowing Lord Winden would approve of a sweet demure smile, she made sure to grin with a rude display of big white teeth. Then, instead of addressing him properly, she said, "Hello, Winnie. Have you been out whipping the world into shape?"

This was intended to offend Lord Winden, who would never bother enough with the world's condition to get out a whip—although he might whip people who called him Winnie instead of Lord Winden.

"Good day, Miss Stratton," he said, smiling. She hated to admit to herself that he had a wonderful smile. "In fine form, as always."

He had not known her always. He had known her only two weeks. He'd attached himself to Father like a son. The only good thing about the man was the hyphen in his first name, Hugh-David. And his authentic title. All Devonny's friends were mad about British titles. Even her father, usually so sensible, had fallen for this person just because of the title.

Of course everybody adored the English. They were so civilized, and had all those sweet things like coats of arms, and castles, and servants. (Devonny had servants, but American servants were immigrants who got tired of it in a week and moved on. In England, people actually liked to be servants, and even trained their children to do it, too.) The best books were by English writers, the most wonderful ceremonies were for the Queen, and the handsomest soldiers in the brightest of uniforms served the British Empire.

But it was one thing to love Britain; it was quite another to love an actual person. There were three Englishmen staying at the Stratton estate that week, and Devonny found them all boring, stupid and useless. Hugh-David and his friends Gordon and Miles did nothing with their lives. They were like women. They thought mainly of Society: what they would wear, whom they would meet, how the flowers would look on the table. Devonny was embarrassed for them.

"You are covered with dust," observed Lord Winden in his charming British accent. "I cannot think what you have been doing, Miss Stratton." Everything the man said was half accusation, as if he hoped to repair Devonny.

"I was admiring the new fountain, Winnie. Have you seen it yet?" Devonny's mansion had been very stylish a decade ago, but styles change. The new fountain would be as magnificent as Rome.

And just as magnificent as Rome were the Italian workmen. It was warm for October, and the men had taken off their shirts. Devonny was still reeling from the sight of a half dozen men with no shirts on. Of course Lord Winden hadn't seen the fountain; he would never walk where workmen labored. Stone dust and sweat and swearing immigrants were not attractive to him.

They were extremely attractive to Flossie, who had

fallen in love with the stone carver's son, Johnny. Flossie was even now huddled behind the lace curtain in the tower room, watching them work. Devonny could hardly wait to get upstairs so she and Flossie could discuss Johnny's bare chest.

Lord Winden, however, wanted to talk.

Devonny felt that people should talk only when she wanted talk, and get out of the way when she wanted them out of the way. Her father said this attitude would not be useful in marriage, but luckily Devonny was barely sixteen, and not considering marriage.

Devonny would fall in love one day like Flossie, and her love, too, would be mad and dangerous and beautiful. But not now. Devonny wanted love, like talk, to come at the exact hour when it would be convenient. Not sooner, and not later.

In the distance, a chestnut mare, ridden by Devonny's stepmother, Florinda, cantered across the meadow. How lovely Florinda was in her black habit, her tall hat, her perfect sidesaddle posture.

Lord Winden's only real interest was horses. Devonny and Lord Winden had gone riding several times, and the advantage was that conversation was limited. Lord Winden's conversation was limited anyhow, so it was a fine arrangement.

"I have not seen the fountain," he conceded. "More attractive than bricklaying, Miss Stratton, would be your father's golf course."

"Do you play golf, Lord Winden?" Devonny thought better of him now that he had a second interest in life.

"Of course. Have you tried it yourself? I have seen ladies on the greens."

Devonny could beat Lord Winden using a tennis racket to hit the golf ball, and she considered explaining this, but decided it was time to practice flirting. If she began now, at sixteen, by the time she came out in two years, she would be excellent, and the young men of Society would swoon in her presence. So she said, "I am sure you are superb." This was a complete lie, but Devonny had observed that this was flirting: lying to men.

She must acquire every skill, because at eighteen, she would be ready for the greatest shopping expedition of all: husband hunting. Since she knew exactly what she wanted, it was just a matter of tracking him down.

"Perhaps this afternoon you and I might enjoy a game of golf," said Lord Winden.

Devonny adored the clothing of golf. Father chose Devonny's wardrobe, and he had forbidden her to wear the new style, which was very plain: long-sleeved white shirt, ankle-length unadorned dark skirt. Devonny loved this style, which felt so businesslike, and brought closer her dream of being a Self-Made Woman.

But in obedience to her father, she wore a flounced yellow and white striped organza gown, cut low to display a smashing necklace. If she agreed to golf, she could put on white stockings, a white skirt that stopped *above her ankles,* and a white blouse with navy trim. A sailor suit. Such was the power of clothing that in so short a dress, Devonny felt swifter and more able.

"I should be delighted," she said, wondering if she should thrash him at golf or let him win. "And now, if you will excuse me, sir . . ."

They bowed to one another, and she sailed indoors, forcing herself to mount the great stair slowly, and with dignity, rather than taking the steps two at a time to get the love letter to Flossie. Oh, it was all so much fun! She doubted if poor old Lord Winden had ever had any fun in his life. She glided under huge portraits of glaring grandparents. She stepped around the great flowing velvet drapes, which lay on the floor like wine-red snowbanks, and reached the next floor. Then she charged down the hall, threw open the tower door, slammed it behind her, raced up the tower stairs and ripped off her glove to give the note to Flossie.

Inside was not just handwriting. Johnny had included a lock of his beautiful curly black hair. Flossie closed her eyes with joy.

I will feel like that someday, thought Devonny.

Bells and stars and fireworks. I, too, will have a keepsake book for the love letters and the curl of hair.

"Do you know how he spells Johnny?" said Flossie dreamily, putting the lock of hair against her lips and kissing it. "G-I-A-N-N-I." She folded the flimsy paper back over the lock of hair, and closed her fingers as if slipping on a wedding ring. "Devonny," she whispered, her smile so pure that Flossie seemed nothing but joy, "I am going to marry him."

Devonny was irked. Johnny was entertainment, nothing more. "Don't be silly, Flossie. Your parents would never speak to you again."

"I shall live with him in his house."

Flossie Van Stead was the fourth daughter in an immensely wealthy family. Her summer cottage was even larger than Devonny's, her yacht longer and her private rail car more sumptuous.

"The Annellos live in a four-family tenement, Flossie. His mother actually cooks the food they eat." It was peculiar food, too, a mushy wormlike dish called macaroni; Johnny had brought it in his lunch pail and neither girl had been willing to taste it. "She washes their clothes, Flossie, in a tub, with her own hands. You can't do that. She shovels the ashes out of the stove!"

Flossie waved this away. "Mama and Papa won't let that happen. Once we're married, they'll give us all the money we need."

"Married!" cried Devonny. "But this is a game! We're just playing."

Flossie lifted Devonny's hands and clasped them between her own. "No," she said, as if from a great distance. "No, dear friend. Johnny and I are not playing."

Devonny shivered at the intensity of Flossie's soft voice.

"Johnny and I are going to elope."

But Flossie's mother and father would not give her all the money she needed. They would not permit her in their house again, nor speak her name, for Johnny was Italian, and Roman Catholic, and poor, and low-class.

Devonny knew well what an angry parent could do. When her own brother, Strat, had disappointed their father, Strat (the only son; the beloved heir) had been locked up in a lunatic asylum. There had been no pity. There had been no discussion.

A failed child was disposed of.

If Strat, so fine and strong and handsome, so bright and capable and affectionate, could be tossed aside like trash into the alley, what would become of Flossie?

"You must help us," whispered Flossie.

Devonny gasped and moved away, touching the panes of the encircling windows, trying to collect her-

10

self. Clouds danced on a brilliant blue sky. The sea shimmered green and foamed white. The woods were scarlet and gold. On such a day, Strat should be here, playing tennis, laughing on the beach, going for a sail.

Whatever had happened to Strat, they would never learn. As the months had gone by without him, hope for Strat had been dashed like seawater on wicked rocks.

They had not found his bones.

Devonny had disobeyed her father many times, but only in small ways: used the telephone without permission; ridden her horse astride like a man; taken off her veil and let the sun beat on her cheeks, risking her greatest asset, her pale complexion. For Flossie to disobey in the matter of a husband—it was unthinkable.

Marry without permission? A Roman Catholic? A laborer? An Italian?

The Van Steads had three other daughters to consider ahead of a foolish one like Flossie, and what was a daughter, anyway, but someone who had not turned out to be a boy? Mr. and Mrs. Van Stead would destroy Flossie as Father had destroyed Strat.

Devonny must prevent this idea of eloping! "Flossie," she began, "he isn't our kind."

"I shall become his kind," said Flossie. Love glowed on her face. Flossie was willing, Flossie was *eager*, to cut off her life. No more Society, no more travel, no more parents and family and friends, no dresses or dancing or parties. Had she no comprehension of what she would lose?

Flossie pointed out the tower window. The men laying stone along the fountain's edge had stopped for a break. They wiped sweat from their foreheads. The afternoon sun beat down, turning their skin copper. Johnny was wandering away from his father and uncles and cousins, sauntering toward the long narrow dirt path that led to the holly garden. There he would wait for Flossie.

Devonny loved that path. On one side, a cliff fell straight down to the ocean, and on the other, high shrubs tickled the passerby with delicate branches. Alone on that path she felt like a frontier woman, her rifle at her side to shoot bears that threatened her babies. Soon the men would widen the path, adding stone walls and little stone lookouts, and the frontier feeling would be ruined.

But if Flossie took that path, *she* would be ruined.

Devonny had known somebody once who had been willing to step across a greater border than Flossie would cross: a girl from another time and place, who had come to save Strat when nothing and no one else could do it.

Was it Devonny's turn now to take a great risk for love, even though it was not her own love? Must she risk all for Flossie? Or should she take the deep and terrible choice of telling on Flossie? Telling in time to prevent such a dreadful act? Would that be love . . . or the terrible betrayal of her most important friendship?

Again she thought of Strat. Annie Lockwood had existed, and Devonny knew that somehow Annie had saved Strat. From this distance, her certainty really did seem lunatic.

And yet . . . she believed. She believed that the love of Annie had rescued her brother.

So Devonny said, in honor of love, "Yes, I will help you, Flossie. Go. Catch up to Johnny. I will keep the household busy."

Below, on the spreading porch, Lord Winden uncovered the letter he had been writing to his mother, the Duchess. He paid no attention to green fields and white-capped ocean. He did not notice the gleaming white veranda floors, the robin's egg blue ceilings and the lacy carved balustrades around him. He continued the second paragraph.

*Americans make me ill. They are in love with money. The price of this, the stock in that. They actually talk about their work as if it's something to be proud of. No one talks about hunting or horses. They jabber about* coal and railroads and hog slaughtering. I would be ashamed to admit that I had anything to do with warehouses.

I know how you feel about Americans, Mama. You are sickened when one duke after another comes home with an American bride.

On the other hand, Mama, those men come home rich. They can now keep the best horses, own a yacht, and enjoy their clubs. I am the fourth son, Mama, and my inheritance is meager. I wish to live well, and that will take money.

It is so easy to impress these people. They love a British accent, and clasp their hands, and beg you to talk more, as if you were an exhibit at a fair. Then they introduce you to their most beautiful young girls.

American girls are loud, pushy, ridiculous — and rich.

I want one who is too young to have become loud and pushy. I want one without a mother, because American mothers are the loudest and pushiest of all.

I have found her.

Her name is Devonny Stratton. Yes — the Stratton railroad fortune.

She is the only child. There was an older brother, but he died in some messy hunting accident. She is the sole heir. Think of the money! She is sixteen, too young to be out in Society, so she knows nothing, which is excellent; you shall train her. Her father (the most uncouth ungentlemanly unattractive American I have

14

*met, and that is saying something) loves my titles, ac-*
*cent, clothing and manners.*

*I shall require that the money comes directly to me.*
*American fathers are touchy about that. As you know,*
*their daughters continue to have control, and problems*
*result. I shall point out how young his daughter is; I*
*must be in charge. So far, he has agreed to everything I*
*have said.*

*There is no need to cross the ocean for the wedding,*
*Mama.*

*She is only an American.*


As Flossie rushed joyfully down the back stairs, Devonny sailed down the front. She slowed to a lady-like pace and prepared herself to keep the gentlemen occupied, to prevent anybody from catching a glimpse of Flossie.

Out on the porch, Lord Winden had been joined by his two useless companions. Devonny paused in front of the huge hall mirror to inspect herself and be sure she did not look as emotional as she felt. Her hair, on which her maid had spent an hour that morning, was fixed in plump ringlets, which gleamed pleasingly in a ray of afternoon sun.

Gordon's voice came clearly through the open screen door. "I will be glad to return home. In this country, one must be polite to so many unpleasant people."

15

"There are uses for Americans," said Miles.

"No," said Hugh-David, "one use. Money."

The men laughed.

The tables were piled with afternoon desserts: cakes and creams and lofty pies with whipped meringues. Flowers were everywhere, and so were bees.

Devonny hoped Hugh-David would get stung.

"Just get her pregnant, have a son and be done with her," came the suggestion.

"I can't put the girl on the shelf that quickly. I'll want a second son," said Hugh-David.

It occurred to Devonny that Flossie would have Johnny's son. She blushed to be thinking of such a thing, but how were sons created? She and Flossie discussed this often, but had come to no conclusions.

Who decided whether a baby would be a boy or a girl? It must be God. If it were up to the husband, no girl would ever be born.

"And Lisette?" said Miles. "Does she know you're taking a bride?"

"Of course. Lisette is delighted," said Hugh-David. "Think of all the Stratton money I can now spend on her."

Stratton money? thought Devonny. She paused, fingertips resting on the glass doorknob.

"American women are difficult about things like this," warned Gordon.

"Miss Stratton is a child. She won't understand,"

said Hugh-David. "But you're quite right, of course. American women are very tedious on the subject of mistresses."

Devonny might be a child, but now she understood all too well. She stormed out onto the porch. "Who do you think you are, you pitiful excuse for a man?" she shouted at Lord Winden.

Three mouths gaped open in shock above their starched collars.

"You can't even earn a living!" yelled Devonny. She felt herself getting taller and thinner, literally towering with rage.

The Englishmen got to their feet quickly, because one stood in the presence of a lady, even a screaming, misbehaving lady.

"You haven't asked me to marry you, Hugh-David Winden, and I wouldn't marry you if you were the last man on earth! I will marry a man with spunk, and you are horse manure!"

Her father's study was very dark.

It was filled with oil paintings, the frames so heavy they seemed to drip gold. Carved gargoyles leered out of the woodwork, and unread books sat locked and cold in glass cabinets.

Devonny's father said softly, in his voice of crushed rocks, and crushed lives, "You will marry him, Devonny."

She was weeping. "Father, you can't mean that."

"Devonny, let us consider the situation once more. Your brother went insane. Insanity is in your blood. Nobody would marry you if this became known, least of all an Englishman with a title. The sons you produce might have bad blood, too. I must marry you off before word of your brother's lunacy spreads. I have agreed to this marriage."

"No, Father! I don't love him. I don't think I could ever grow to love him!"

"Love is not a concern," said her father. "I have agreed to the marriage, and I have agreed that it will happen now."

"*Now?* Father, I haven't even entered Society yet. It's unseemly to arrange a marriage when I am so young. People will think that—that—" Devonny could not speak of the conception of babies with her stepmother, never mind her father. She rallied. "Father, first let me tell you my own plans."

Her father took her chin in his huge hand and turned her face roughly back and forth to remind her that she was an object, which he could position any way he chose. Her tears ran down his thick fingers. "I have told you what the plans are, daughter."

His vest was sprung tight over his spreading flesh. Pipe smoke surrounded him in a choking cloud.

"Father," she said desperately. It was difficult to

speak with her jaw caught in his grip, difficult to think as her eyes were being flung from one direction to the other. "I have been considering telephones. Only five years ago, we had never utilized such a machine. Now, in New York City, there are tens of thousands of instruments. Father, I believe the future of America lies not in railroads, not in ocean shipping, but in telephones!"

He let go of her with a sort of thrust, half jamming her jaw back into the throat. Devonny kept on. "Sir, I wish to begin telephone service to—"

"Your purpose," said her father in a voice of iron, the iron in which he had made his fortune, "is to become an obedient wife. You will not shame me again in front of my guests. I have not permitted you to acquire blemishes on your complexion and I will not permit you to acquire blemishes in your behavior."

The rage was in his hands, the hands becoming fists. Devonny must calm him down, make a friend of him again. "Father, how can you have respect for Hugh-David when he isn't capable of running a business? He can ride a horse, visit his club and use a tennis racket. Why are you not contemptuous of him?"

"He's an Englishman," said her father. "One doesn't expect accomplishments from them. But you'll have a title, and your son—*my grandson*—will sit in Parliament." Her father laughed. It was a thick cruel chuckle. "In fact, at the rate these penniless dukes are snapping up American brides, many sons of America will sit in Parliament. American grandsons will rule England." With his heavy drooping mustache and grizzled beard, he looked like an ancient ape. "A half-breed, the English will call your son. They have no use for Americans; they might as well be marrying a savage. But how they love our money. And you, my dear, come with a large supply."

Well, she was not going to marry Hugh-David, who had a mistress and scorned Americans! It was out of the question! Why, Flossie marrying Johnny was better off!

But her father was dreaming of grandsons. To supply them, she must wed somebody else. "I could marry Randal," she offered.

Her father snorted. "That simpleton?" He handed Devonny an envelope. Devonny opened the letter slowly, understanding that Randal, whose silence had hurt, had written to her after all. Father had chosen to keep Devonny's mail.

*My dearest Devonny,*
    *Thank you for so many lovely visits while we were in California. Of course I had hoped to see more of you,*

*but it is not to be. I congratulate you on your upcoming marriage. Perhaps our paths will cross while you are on your wedding trip in Europe.*

*Ever your respectful friend,*
*Randal Porter, Esq.*

Devonny tore the letter in half and carefully fed the halves to the fire, to prevent herself from saving the letter and weeping over it. "Father," she said, for she knew this parent well, "did you pay him?"

Father picked up his pipe and chewed slowly on the end of it. Devonny envied him. Smoking a pipe gave a gentleman so much to do—filling, tamping, lighting, puffing—while she could only stand quietly, awaiting his pleasure. At least she had control over her tears now. Her neck hurt from being wrenched back and forth, but she would not massage the ache lest her father take satisfaction from it.

"Devonny, I have groomed you to be a good wife. Now," he said, "your breeding must show."

He purposely used words meant for horses. Groomed. Breeding.

I am nothing, she thought, but breeding stock. "Father, I know you care about my happiness." She did not know this. Father had never shown a particle of interest in her happiness.

"Your happiness consists of pleasing me."

"But Father—"

"Do not begin another sentence with the word but." He advanced, and she knew the slap was coming, but held still, hoping he would recall that complexions were everything; a bruise on her face would not be attractive.

They stared at each other.

She could only hope that Lord Winden would be so humiliated by her shrieking in front of his friends that he was already packing, off to find a bride with better manners.

Her father lifted the leather rectangle that lay on his massive desk. Into its triangular corners, a new blotter was fitted every morning. Flat and hidden underneath lay a single piece of ivory paper with rippled edges.

"Read it," he said. Fury mottled his speech. So this piece of paper was the source of his recent rage. It could not be a letter from Johnny Annello; he wrote on cheap lined school pads. It could not be from Flossie; she used Devonny's onionskin paper.

Devonny was afraid to reach for it, lest her father stab her hand with the letter opener and pin her to the desk. What could be on that page, to turn her father into a beast?

The writing was copperplate, that slender elegant script used by educated people. Spidery letters wove delicately over the page.

*Your only son died insane, Mr. Stratton. Your daughter carries the blood of insanity. Devonny may receive offers of marriage . . . but if I produce papers you signed, committing your son to the Evergreen Asylum for the Insane, your daughter will die a spinster. No grandson for you. No next generation to inherit the fortune you created. Unless, of course, you wish to purchase that paper from me . . . and if so, you must act quickly, for there are other interested parties.*

Devonny was gasping for air. *Blackmail.* The corset that reduced her twenty-three-inch waist to eighteen inches allowed no room for frightened lungs. *To die a spinster.* Devonny could think of no worse prison.

"The writer of this letter," said her father, measuring his syllables to keep the rage from corrupting them, "has chosen a good year. There is nothing happening in New York City. Newspaper readers are bored by descriptions of children in tenements and senators taking graft. Insanity in my family would delight reporters. It would destroy my chances of marrying you off at all, let alone having you marry well."

Devonny examined the letter for clues, turning it over, and over again, as if she would find a signature, or an address, or a clue. "Do you know who wrote the letter, Father?"

"If I knew, he would be at the bottom of the

ocean," said her father. "But I shall find out. No one threatens me."

It was true. Father had smashed unions rather than raise pay or cut hours. He had closed a plant, losing huge sums of money, rather than acknowledge the union trying to form there. When renters of his tenements were late with payments, they were removed by force, even if the woman was in labor or the husband dying. As for how Father had treated Mother, had treated Strat—these hardly bore thinking of.

But for once, Devonny was glad for her father's roughness. *Blackmail!* Yes, that person must be destroyed! And who better than Father to crush someone?

"It is imperative to get you wed, on a ship out of the country, and with child. Lord Winden is in a hurry to be rich, and I am in a hurry to get you married. It is a good match. We will have your wedding within the month."

Devonny nearly fainted. She had dreamed of her wedding day all her life. Nobody could put together a wedding in a month! A month wasn't time to arrange bridesmaids, have bridal teas, and—

"We will borrow a wedding gown," said her father, "and put my New York staff to work on the reception."

*Borrow a wedding gown?*

Devonny wanted to scream or weep. At least, if she

24

must be married off like this, the wedding gown should be her choice! It should be designed just for her, they should send to Paris for it, she ought to have . . .

But whatever she ought to have, she would not.

She, Devonny Aurelia Victoria Stratton, would reach not a single one of her dreams. Instead, she would have an unwanted marriage, years too early. A man who despised her family. A life in a foreign land among foreign people.

Her father slipped the letter carefully into its hiding place. Devonny was amused. The servants who changed that blotter and polished that desk had probably memorized the contents and told the entire household. There were few secrets in a mansion run by servants. How amazing that her father, who knew everything, did not know this.

"You will go now," said her father, "and apologize to your future husband. Explain that you behaved badly, but it is merely youth. You have much to learn, and you hope he will be kind enough to forgive you. You hope for his thoughtful control over your person, so that you will behave better in the future."

"Father," she said, groping for a strategy to combat this, or at least stall it.

"Or," said her father, leaning so close to Devonny that the bristly edges of his beard scraped her cheek, "I will tell Hugh-David myself. Her brother is insane,

25

I will explain. I cannot permit her to contaminate this world with insane children, I will tell him." Her father expelled a lungful of cigar smoke into her eyes. "The wedding, I will announce, is off."

Devonny pressed her hands to her eyes.

"You will then choose a bedroom, Devonny, and in that room you will spend the remainder of your days."

Hiram Stratton's past was strewn with the ruined lives of people who had offended him. Hiram Stratton did not joke and Hiram Stratton did not exaggerate.

So Devonny went to Lord Winden, pale and trembling, as a woman should be.

He was kind, however, and said that he understood. She had been shocked, he agreed, and ladies did not manage surprises well. Their weak systems could not tolerate confusion. Devonny was not to feel shame. He would make all decisions in the future. She was to stay out of the sun and keep her lovely complexion, because such fair skin would please his mother, the Duchess.

"Thank you for your greatness of heart, sir," said Devonny, who would rather have put a knife through him, and he said, "Good girl," and they went together to her father, to ask his blessing on their marriage.

"First," said Lord Winden, using his cute little accent, playing with his cute little mustache, "we shall discuss the contract."

Devonny was sent away. The men would handle her life and fortune without her.

And so it was, on a beautiful windy day in October 1898, that Devonny Aurelia Victoria Stratton went alone to a remote corner of the Stratton estate, where she knelt and begged for rescue, as if she really thought a gracious God or a knight in shining armor might come for her.

# TWO

*Of* course a man making his fortune could not be expected to show up for his junior year in high school. Tod Lockwood was disgusted when his parents, principal, teachers and even neighbors did expect just that.

"In the olden days," Tod explained crossly, "a boy quit school in the eighth grade and went out and made his fortune."

"How olden are you getting?" his father asked. "That's more olden than I ever was. You're going back a century."

Tod felt there had been many possibilities to the nineteenth century. Men were men. Fortunes were waiting to be made in railroads and shipping and automobiles.

Tod had to live in an era of computer keyboards. Tod got bored sitting still that long. He did not want to spend his life typing.

Luckily, he had a truly brilliant idea: designer water.

People were thrilled by water in bottles. Tod couldn't figure out what they saw in those bottles, other than water, but they sure did, and they sure paid for it. How many businesses were there where all you needed up front were some bottles and your own faucet?

Of course Tod's Kitchen Tap Water probably wouldn't sell. So he was taking the water from the spring at Stratton Point, an old waterfront estate that was now the town beach. Over the spring was the original pump, with a curved red handle, which had to be pumped several times to get the pressure up. Then Tod had to lug all those gallons of water away. How many times did a person want to hang around the picnic grounds pumping water by hand?

Once.

So Tod was diluting the water from the spring at Stratton Point with his kitchen tap water, and it tasted just fine.

An artsy friend designed a label for his bottles: pine trees (Stratton Point didn't have any), a romantic mansion (the Stratton mansion had been torn down), and a sweet tumbling brook (the water came out of a rusty pump). According to business magazines, red was a selling color, right up there with cobalt blue. He was going with red. He obtained several thousand eight-ounce plastic bottles and spent happy hours sticking labels on them.

The designer water business gave Tod plenty to think about when he was home. His parents had gotten back together, so thoroughly that they were having a second honeymoon right there in the house. They were so mushy Tod had to spend all his time with his face averted.

Sure, Tod was glad the family was back together and all that stuff, but he wished they weren't *this* together. It was embarrassing. Tod wished he lived in a time when men led their lives and women led theirs, and nobody had to pay attention, or make an effort, or compromise.

He used to have an ally of sorts: his sister, Annie. Annie and Tod had never gotten along well, but they got along somewhat, in certain circumstances. But Annie had a chance to spend a semester abroad and was in Norway, while he was bottling water and watching his parents smooch.

Then the water didn't sell.

It turned out there was a lot of competition in the bottled water business. This was discouraging for an afternoon, and then Tod realized that he had to do some serious marketing. The first thing to do was to increase demand for water. People had to drink more of it.

He was going to hire pretty girls in tights and spangles to sell his water at the high school, but the principal said this was sexist—plus school was not about sales, it was about knowledge.

Then he decided to convince people that cafeteria liquids (milk, soda, iced tea) were defective, and gave you disease, and you'd better buy Stratton Point Spring Water. The cafeteria ladies threatened to beat him up.

Okay, fine. If people wouldn't drink it, they'd wash in it. He'd sell it in the chemistry and biology labs. "Your hands are safer from acids and frog blood if bathed in Stratton Point Spring Water."

It turned out that people who were willing to pay almost two dollars to drink water were not willing to pay to wash their hands in it. Tod tried to point out how stupid this was, but the class told him to get lost, and take his water with him.

Well, there were always tourists.

Tod went downtown among the leaf peepers—in October, New England was full of tourists from the rest of the United States, Europe and Japan—and hawked his water. At last! Success! Foreigners who did not know much about water in the United States were delighted with this souvenir. Tod's former scoutmaster, a man who lived up to being clean, strong, honest and true, said if Tod didn't give back the right change, he was a dead ex-Scout. This cut Tod's income, but still, he sold every bottle in one weekend.

So Tod went down to Stratton Point to get more spring water, because what with scoutmasters on his case, he had to have at least a drop or two of the real thing in each bottle.

Tod was not thinking of love.

Tod did not have a whole lot of use for love, being more interested in money. Besides, love involved girls, and Tod was not that drawn to girls. They giggled; they resembled his sister and mother, who were extremely difficult human beings to understand. Tod figured when he was thirty and a millionaire, established in the world and driving several cars, maybe racing them, there would be time for love. No need to rush it.

Carefully arranging her enormous skirts to prevent grass stains, Devonny Stratton went down on her knees and prayed for rescue. All brides forced into weddings pray for rescue. But there could be none, for only a man could rescue a woman, and the man in Devonny's life had arranged the marriage.

Far across the meadows, the three towers of the Mansion glinted in the sun. Between Devonny and that imposing silhouette were hundreds of elm, chestnut, maple and oak trees, brilliant October blurs of scarlet, gold and yellow. What a contrast was the dark cold green of the holly garden where Flossie and Johnny had dared snatch a moment.

By now, Flossie would be back at the house, probably agreeing to golf with Gordon or Miles. Her flushed cheeks and pounding heart would not betray her, for Gordon and Miles were so proud that each man would think himself responsible.

Devonny too must return to the house with nothing in manner or speech that could betray her. Fury and fear alternated in her heart. Fear won.

The next few years should have been such fun! Her girlfriends and Strat's buddies from college—laughing, rowing across the little lake, having clambakes, dancing in the ballroom, acting out plays, and laughing again.

And it was not to be.

"Mama," she said brokenly, though she hardly knew her mother. The two children had been kept by Father when he divorced and began his string of remarriages. Mama lived in poverty, with barely enough to keep warm in winter, never mind stay in fashion, and give parties for friends.

Devonny thought bleakly of her mother's awful dark little house in Brooklyn, only one room heated in winter; only one servant to help. How could Flossie possibly find romance in poverty?

In all these years, Mama had found no way around poverty, and if she could not help herself, she certainly could not help Devonny. Mama had not been able to help Strat either, though she had tried.

33

Father was lying to Lord Winden about Strat's end, claiming that Strat died in a hunting accident in the mountains. But they did not know that. Strat had vanished. That was all they knew.

Devonny herself had given an order to Annie Lockwood: If you have no other way to save Strat, bring him with you into your own century.

It was such a strange thought: that Strat might be out there—breathing, running, laughing, reading the paper—but not for a hundred years.

*What if Strat came back?*

The question of money would also come back. If Father's only son returned, it would be much less likely that Devonny would inherit everything. And much less likely that Lord Winden would want Devonny. In fact, Lord Winden would *not* want Devonny!

As for Father's threat . . . forbidden to marry; a useless dried-up old spinster kept in a separate room . . . if I could get Strat home, thought Devonny, I could prove he is no lunatic. Then there could be no blackmail! And Strat would take care of me. He's a man now, and would overrule Father. I would not be thrown into a marriage like a ball into a game! I could marry for love.

*I must bring Strat home.*

Devonny straightened the long glimmering yellow skirt. She retied the lovely sash. She touched the

34

cameo at her throat. She felt the freshness of the flowers on her hat.

How had they done it?

How had they stepped through?

What magic word, or place, or thought, or need had ripped her brother and Annie Lockwood through a century?

"Strat!" she cried. "Strat! I need you!"

But nothing happened.

Devonny stomped her small foot, but her soft leather sole made hardly a sound in the high grass. She did not even have the power to make noise.

There was no Annie Lockwood. There was no Strat. In fact, what her father had told Lord Winden was probably the truth: that Strat was dead in the mountains.

"Somebody help me," said Devonny tonelessly. She did not raise her voice. "Somebody think of something to do," she said, not loud enough to make a swallow change flight.

She shaded her eyes to see the nearest village on the shore. Was Strat there? Just a few miles away— and a hundred years?

If she stepped through, as somehow they had stepped through, could she find him? Would he be waiting for her? Would he even know her?

Devonny clasped her hands and held them before her. She addressed Time, which held Strat: *I need him,* she said, *take me to him. I have no power. Only my brother can save me.*

Tod put his mouth to the spigot and drank several cooling gulps. He never worried about stuff like germs or dirt. When he got a mouthful of rust, he just swallowed it. Tod never got sick. It was a matter of choice. You wanted to stay well, you informed your body, and it obeyed you.

Within seconds, Tod was hideously sick.

His head was coming off. His whole body was being wrenched apart.

Tod had never even had the flu. He could not imagine what was happening. He wanted to throw up, or grab on to something, or scream, but there was no Time.

Time, he thought; and somehow, grotesquely, *he could touch time.*

Time, which was invisible, like love or power, pressed up against him, and scraped his skin, and tried to break his bones.

Tod tried to brush it off himself, as if he'd walked into spiderwebs, but he had no control over his hands, and then his hair peeled away as if he were being scalped.

There was so much Time.

Years and decades of Time, fat swollen hours of

Time, like disease. The sickness lasted a century, and yet used up no Time at all.

Then came the after-feeling of sickness: a thin brain and a weak belly. Tod found himself still gripping the red-handled pump, still kneeling on the soggy grass.

He tried to breathe deeply but his body was unwilling. He panted in a shallow fashion and forced his hand to relax on the pump handle. A drop of water lay neatly on the rim of the spigot. It grew larger, and fell. The paint was not peeling. The red was shiny, as if painted that morning. There was no rust around the iron rim. In fact, beautiful brass trim covered the place where Tod had just put his lips.

What if the water's poisonous? he thought. Oh, that'll be great. I can't wait to announce that downtown. You know those tourists who overpaid for my bottled water? Well, get the hospital beds ready. . . .

Using the pump for support, Tod stumbled to his feet. He felt disoriented, or else carsick.

A girl was standing there. He didn't remember running into anybody else at Stratton Point.

But this was not anybody.

She wore an enormous dress, yellow satiny stuff cascading all around her. She had really strange shoes on — but then, Tod's mother often wore shoes that a normal human would never shove over his toes. She had on an amazing necklace — but then, Tod's sister wore necklaces made of anything from crystals to plastic bear claws. This girl's hair, however, was in a class by itself. Long separate cylinders jostled for space on her shoulders and delicate tiny wisps lay sweetly on her cheeks and forehead.

I'm in the middle of a photo shoot, he thought.

The girl was staring at him with an incredulous expression, and now she was extending her hands, slow motion, as if she wanted to dance. "Yeah. Hi," he said nervously. "How are ya? I'm outta here, sorry I interrupted." He looked around to see the camera crew and retrieve the water carrier.

No camera crew. No water carrier.

No picnic ground. No parking lot. No car.

In fact, no road.

The sickness rolled over him again, and he focused once more on the girl. She was very pretty, although Tod tried not to judge these things; it just got him interested in the girl, and he was not ready to allocate time to girls. She was laughing, she was coming toward him, it was some creepy joke, it was—

She hugged him.

Tod had never had a girlfriend. Never been hugged by any female person except a relative, and then usually under orders. She was amazingly soft. She was definitely and completely not a boy.

She was laughing with delight. "Who are you?" She released him. "I'm Devonny. Have you come for me? Is Strat with you? How did you do it? I am so happy to see you! How are you going to save me?"

"What?" said Tod, feeling that his life had just come apart in some essential way. "I'm Tod Lockwood," he said, because he was still sure of that.

"Annie's brother!" she cried, clapping her hands.

She was wearing gloves. Tod had never seen anything so strange in his life. The gloves were lace and her real fingertips stuck out. Around her wrists the lace was gathered with living flowers, a sort of rose bracelet. The lace muffled her clap, giving it a strange, indoor sound.

"Annie sent you," she said joyfully.

Tod felt marginally better. It was not surprising that his sister, who was nuts, would have friends who were nuts and dressed crazy. "Nope, Annie's still in Norway," he said. "This is my own business. I sell bottled water."

A lace hand flew to her mouth and an expression of horror crossed the girl's face. "What do you mean, Annie's in Norway?"

"Well, you know, she got accepted in a student exchange, and she'll be in Scandinavia for six months. Then we take an exchange student in our house. She'll be back in February."

"She sent you instead, then," said the girl, and her smile became peaceful. "I," said the girl, "am Devonny Stratton."

"Cool. I didn't know there were any Strattons left," he said. He kind of liked the name Devonny. "Town's owned the place for fifty years."

"What place?" she said.

Yes, undoubtedly a friend of Annie's. They were nothing but computer errors, Annie's friends. Or viruses, depending on his mood.

That had been some drink of water.

Tod knew every inch of Stratton Point, all two hundred acres. Like every kid in town, he loved the Point. The beaches were best, but everything from holly garden to bell tower was his, by exploration and childhood. All those neat places where the Stratton family had had fountains, lookouts and stables all those years ago.

And yet, Tod did not know where he was standing. The sick feeling swirled through his head. His thoughts fogged up like a windshield. He, who knew every square foot of Stratton Point, could recognize nothing. Where was the road? Where was the car?

"I did not even know about you, Mr. Lockwood," said Devonny Stratton. "Your sister never mentioned you."

*Mr.* Lockwood? "I don't mention her either, if I can help it," said Tod.

"Is Strat living with you?" said the girl anxiously. "Did Annie bring Strat home with her?"

"We only have one pet right now," said Tod. "A

collie named Cotton. Listen, I'm feeling a little strange. Like, where are we, exactly?"

There was a long silence.

Tod had never known such silence. Not just the girl refusing to speak—*but the world.* No cars, no engines, no planes, no radios . . . He turned in a long, slow, full circle. There, on the Great Hill, stood the Mansion. Not the crumbling hulk the town had demolished last year. But a magnificent glittering three-towered—

—*new* building.

The peeled sensation came back, as if his brain tissue had been left open to the air.

"You have come to me," said Devonny Stratton slowly, "in my Time. The year is 1898," she said, "and you are on my estate."

"Get out of town," said Tod.

But memory was thick and suffocating in his brain. One time his sister had gone missing. Family and friends, and later police, had searched for Annie; searched every corner of this very beach and park, where she had last been seen. There had been no trace of her.

When she had showed up—*two days later!*—his parents had allowed her to get away with the flimsiest excuse: "I fell asleep on the sand," Annie had said.

Had Annie, too, pressed her mouth to this pump?

A muffled cloppy rhythmic sound interrupted the

silence. Through a meadow of asters and high grass came a woman on horseback. The woman was wearing a skirt, long and black, and rode sidesaddle.

Eighteen ninety-eight, thought Tod. He was furious and scared and having a little trouble breathing. No wonder Annie had not been able to think of a good excuse for being away a few days. "I bet my sister loved this, huh, Devonny? She's just the type." Tod was not the type.

"She fell in love," said Devonny, "with my brother, Strat. She came back a final time to rescue Strat from a terrible fate."

Maybe if Tod sort of skidded along the surface here, pretended this was virtual reality, he could flick a switch and be done.

"You must take me with you," said the girl. "My brother must be with you. Annie must have brought him home. I need him. He must save me."

"No," said Tod. "She hasn't dated anybody this year. She sure hasn't brought anybody home. I don't even know anybody named Strat."

The girl began to cry.

Tod hated that; it was a crummy trick. "Don't do that," he snapped. "What does Strat need to save you from? Don't even think about crying. Just give me facts."

"Marriage," she said. "My father has chosen a

dreadful man for me to marry. A man with—well, evil personal habits. A man who wants only my money."

"So?" said Tod. "Just don't marry the guy. Just say no."

She looked at him.

"It's a big slogan in my day, Devonny. If somebody offers you drugs or sex or crime, you just say no."

"I am not in a position to say no to my father," said the girl.

"Sure you are. It's America. Just say no."

"But I am a girl."

He was irritated. "Big deal. You're half the population. Say yes, say no, make up your mind, I don't see what your father has to do with it."

"It would not work. There are complexities. There is blackmail, and there are fortunes, and you are being as annoying as your sister. I need my brother, and I know you have him! Now take me home with you!"

Take you home with me? thought Tod. Yeah, right. Like I'm gonna walk in the door to my house with a teenage girl in a long yellow prom dress and tell my mother we're saving her from a bad marriage.

Tod aimed for control over his blood and bone and brain tissue. Keeping himself unreachable, so he could just slide home, like a baseball player, he said, "Devonny, I can't take you home. And I don't think Annie brought your brother home. Unless he's invisible. And even then, I don't think she'd go off to Norway if she had some cute guy around." He stepped backward, hoping to be on a parking lot again, with his car behind him.

Didn't happen.

"Even now my father and Lord Winden are drawing up a contract to dispose of my assets, Mr. Lockwood. I will be forced into a wedding in only a month."

"What do you mean, dispose of your assets?"

"The opening settlement will be two million dollars for Lord Winden."

"Wow. That should be enough to go around. Tell your father you want it. What could he do?"

"Mr. Lockwood, you are not listening! He can do anything he wishes. I can do nothing. I need Strat."

"What could Strat do that you can't?"

"He's a boy."

"You better not let my mother hear you talk like that, Dev," said Tod. "She'd string you up. She hates when women have a poor self-image."

"I would love to hear your mother's advice," said Devonny. To his absolute horror, she knelt before him and clung to his hands. Her rose bracelet brushed his wrist. He could not bear the sight of her on her knees.

"Take me back with you," she cried, "and together we'll find Strat. Then Strat and I will return to our

Time and he will solve the nightmare in which I am caught."

Tod felt cornered out here in a meadow with nothing in sight but grass and flowers.

"I'd stay in one of your guest rooms," pleaded Devonny. "One of your extra maids could wait on me. You wouldn't even have to seat me at your dining table. The footman could serve me in my room. Mr. Lockwood, I do beg of you."

"Dude," said Tod. He blinked a few times. "Listen, Dev, if you have all this money, you don't need anybody to bail you out. Just get your own house, buy your own car, pay your own insurance, and hey— you're set."

"Oh, this is just like talking to your sister! Annie was so difficult, Mr. Lockwood. Your sister was obstructive and annoying."

"It's good we agree on something. Now you gotta call me Tod."

She shook her head, which caused the long exotic curls to shake, and he wanted to run his finger up inside the cylinders of hair, and then he felt sick all over again, but it was not seasick, or carsick, it was some other sick entirely.

"We haven't been introduced," she said primly.

He yanked her to her feet. "Tod, Devonny. Devonny, Tod. There. We've been introduced. But even introduced, Dev, it wouldn't work. I mean, like,

45

my mom has better things to do. It would all be on me, and I personally don't even like taking the dog for a walk."

"Please, Mr. Lockwood. I must find my brother. He is my only hope!"

"Listen, Devonny, he isn't there. As for me, I've started a new business and I've just figured out how to make money at it. I have customers now, and things to do. Bank accounts to open."

"That's wonderful!" cried Devonny. "I love men like that." She looked at him worshipfully. Never had a girl gazed at him like that. It wasn't too bad.

"I shall join you as soon as I pack my trunk," Devonny said breathlessly. "I know this is why Time brought you to me, Mr. Lockwood."

Tod tried to imagine Devonny in the school cafeteria. In an age of unruly hair, hers was a work of art. In an age of dirty heavy sneakers, she wore white slippers. In an age of torn jeans and obscene T-shirts, she carried a parasol. "What would we tell people? Especially my parents. Dev, you don't wanna marry the guy, don't marry the guy."

"It isn't that simple," protested Devonny, crying again. Tod figured now her mascara would run and her makeup would look crummy, but then he realized that she wasn't wearing makeup. He liked her for that. The whole face correction idea seemed pathetic and ridiculous to Tod. When the girls in school covered themselves with makeup, or when his mother and sister did, he made a point of gagging in front of them.

"I'm gonna leave now," said Tod. Assuming I can, he thought. What if Time decides?

Tod was against that. A person should have complete control over his life. Well, I do, he told himself. I can do anything my sister can do, and she made it back and forth.

"I thought you would be a knight in shining armor," said Devonny. She did not touch her tears, but let them lie on her cheek and throat. "I thought you would save me. Why did you come if you weren't going to save me?"

"It isn't like I meant to come," said Tod.

She looked stricken. As if he had slapped her. Fleetingly, Tod considered what his mother would do to him were he ever to raise a hand to a girl.

He didn't want any heavy thoughts here, or any responsibility. People had to be responsible for themselves. "You don't need saving, Devonny. You just need guts." Tod had no sympathy for weakness. "I'm going," he told her.

She held out her hands, and the flowery bracelet fell from one wrist, and her voice trembled on, saying more, but he stepped back, grabbed the pump handle, closed his eyes—and it worked. Her words followed, crying without sound, *But I need you!*

The pain was worse this time. His vision and hearing and touch were torn apart and savaged. It went on and on, beyond counting, beyond belief. Through it all came the distorted syllables, jumbled and wrecked; *But I need you!*

It was not going to end. He had refused help to a person who needed it, and this would be his hell: falling through the years, unable to get off at one of them.

Time let him hit the edge of every stone and cliff.

He was not alone in this passage. Other bodies and souls, shot with pain, were thrust past him and through him.

But it ended.

His eyes burned, as if he'd ignored sunglasses during a whole day of lying on the beach. When he managed to focus, an old pump, its paint peeling, was next to him, surrounded by plastic containers.

His head throbbed. He hoped aspirin was in the car. He hoped aspirin worked in situations like this.

Tod looked toward the grass on which a girl had begged for help—his help—but there was no grass. Just a parking lot. No girl. Just his own car.

Drops trickled from the rusty edge of the open spigot.

Maybe he should drop the whole designer water idea.

There *was* something in this water.

48

# THREE

The meadow stretched to the sea. Tall grass, blown down by the wind, lay rumpled like a bed. Clouds scudded into other lives, to hang above other eyes.

Had a boy in strange crude clothing, using strange rude speech, spun briefly through Time just to tell her, "No, nobody will save you"?

Devonny stepped toward the pump, to touch it, and then snatched her hand back, as if it might burn. If she had made up that moment with Mr. Lockwood, perhaps there *was* insanity in the Stratton blood.

She did not hear the clomping of horses coming, nor their windy breath, nor the gentle squeaking of leather saddles, nor the voices of the riders. When a hand touched her shoulder, Devonny cried out, spinning around, ready to fend off another century.

Lord Winden was staring at her.

And Gordon and Miles, with Flossie and a friend she had not expected today, Rose. How splendid they

49

looked, in their formal riding costumes. And how foreign; how unknown to her. She thought: Am I half in Mr. Lockwood's century? Am I entirely here?

But that way lay madness.

Rose dismounted and rushed to Devonny to hug and kiss her. It felt strange and wrong. What had Tod Lockwood done to her? What veil or mist had he dropped that she could not quite rejoin her time?

"Oh, Devonny!" cried Rose. Her voice was loud and brittle. Devonny wanted to step away from it. "Such news! So thrilling!"

"What news?" she said.

Rose giggled. "Silly girl. That you and darling Lord Winden will be married! Oh, Devonny, I am so happy for you! Lord Winden has been telling us about his magnificent estate. Devvy, it has two hundred rooms."

"And no plumbing," teased Flossie. Her eyes met Devonny's and they tried to exchange messages, but Flossie's situation was too complex; they needed time together, and words.

"And in need of a new slate roof," agreed Lord Winden. "But my bride and I shall remedy such problems."

At least Devonny would know where her money was going.

"What are you doing here, so far from the house?" asked Rose. "This is such a remote little spot."

50

"On the contrary," said Devonny, "it has a beautiful view. When we were little, Strat and I often played in this meadow." This was untrue. When they were little, Devonny and Strat could not stand each other, and would never have dreamed of spending an instant in each other's company.

Devonny saw that she was going to construct a false childhood to tell Lord Winden, because she did not want him to have any part of her. But he will have part of me, she thought. That is marriage.

Far away, on the narrow gravel road that was the only entrance to the Stratton estate, clattered a large open cart, pulled by two extremely heavy, slow horses. Men sat on the open cart, legs dangling. The syllables of their foreign tongue were faintly audible.

Flossie said, "The stonecutters are done, Devonny. The fountain is complete."

If the stonework was done, Johnny would not return in that cart tomorrow. How would the lovers meet? Was it Devonny's responsibility to ensure that Flossie and her beloved had time together?

Time.

Who, and what, was Time?

"The turf has arrived," said Flossie, as if either she or Devonny cared about this, "and the gardeners are unrolling it. Your dear father expects to turn the water on shortly. We shall have a garden party this evening to celebrate the beauty of the spraying fountain."

"And the joy of our upcoming nuptials," said Lord Winden. He linked his arm in Devonny's. "Miles, take my horse back with you. Miss Stratton and I will walk."

The rest of the party rode away. She was alone with him. A strange man from a strange country. Her fingers tightened on his arm, to hold herself up, and he liked that, and patted her hand. Devonny wanted to sob. Unlike Tod, Lord Winden would be pleased, because female weakness was pleasing to a man in Devonny's century.

It is the only century I have, she thought. If I do as that boy suggested and just say no, I will be a spinster. A thin beaten woman, alone with a needle and thread. Defective. People might study me briefly to see what's wrong with me, but then they'll laugh, and turn away, and occupy themselves with interesting people. "Why don't you marry an English girl, Winnie?"

He smiled at her. A smile she would share with Lisette. "I fear," said Hugh-David, "that English girls who are suitable are as penniless as I."

"An English girl would understand how you live and what the rules are, Winnie."

"I shall teach you the rules. Your father assures me that you comprehend your marriage vows. You will obey me."

The meadow went steeply uphill. She caught her skirts in her right hand, to keep from tripping. "The Stratton family, by and large, does not care for obedience, Winnie. One does not accumulate millions of dollars by obeying."

"The first thing in which you will obey is this, Miss Stratton. You will not address me as Winnie."

"I think it's a sweet nickname."

"No, you don't. You think it will provoke me, and you are correct. Do not use it again."

She saw their lives together. A verbal battle, in which she must always surrender. She would address him as "sir," then, as if he were a stranger at a ball. "How old are you, sir?"

"I am thirty," he said, and to Devonny this was as terrifying as another century.

"I am afraid," she admitted, and hated herself for it.

"You are very young. But you will love England. My mother is difficult, but if you leave all decisions to her, and if she continues to run the houses herself, you will have no problems. And because you are very beautiful, Society will accept you in spite of your being an American."

Society, in London and New York, worshipped beauty. They painted, photographed, wrote about and loved a beautiful girl.

"It's pagan, isn't it?" said Devonny. "If we were

really Christian, we would not care about beauty. But we are not Christian. We worship the body. We adore a beautiful face. It, and not God, is first."

He was shocked. "Of course we are Christian!"

"We go to church," agreed Devonny.

They were the same height, and their eyes met. He had beautiful eyes: large and gray and calm, with long lashes and straight-across eyebrows.

She said, "I don't want to wear a borrowed gown meant for somebody else. I might end up in a life meant for somebody else. I even think you want somebody else."

"My dear, if I were not in great need of money, I should not be taking this step. Winden is not an easy house to maintain. I must put coal in fifty fireplaces, pension my old gamekeepers and nannies, pay cooks and scullery maids, gardeners and yardmen and stable hands. I must maintain carriages and horses." He smiled again. His was a useful smile, much like a signature on the bottom of a contract. "Think of this as your gift to English civilization. You, and you alone, will save this piece of history, Winden Castle."

"I am so sorry," said Devonny, "that the many civil wars of England did not result in the destruction of Winden Castle."

He burst out laughing.

His laugh was as charming as his accent, and she

nearly caved in, nearly let herself like him a little, but she reminded herself that in his description of expenses, Lord Winden was leaving out a great deal. He must have his own tailor, of course, and gambling money. He must have his mistress, and she must have jewels and pleasures. He must be able to go to Paris or even India when the mood took him. And would Devonny go along, or would he leave her with his difficult mother at this castle with its leaking roof and no plumbing?

"It will not be so unhappy as you picture it," he said to her. "I will not be unfair."

Flossie will elope for true love, thought Devonny, and I will wed a man who will not be unfair. "After we are wed," she said tiredly, "when will we make our first visit back to America?"

"Back to America?" he said incredulously. "My dear, once is enough."

The sun was setting. The newly laid turf was emerald green and the sky a painting in purple.

The entire party—her father and stepmother, Florinda; Flossie and her parents, Mr. and Mrs. Van Stead; Rose; and the three Englishmen, Lord Winden, Gordon and Miles—gathered around the new fountain.

Little boys carved of stone cavorted beneath spray

that came from the mouths of dolphins. Circles of sparkling water were tossed into the air, and a spout rose in the middle, casting delicate rainbows.

"And now," said Lord Winden, "another thing of great beauty. It sparkles almost as much, Mr. Stratton, as your fountain."

He opened an old leather box held like a platter on the palms of his manservant's hands.

Resting on ancient crushed velvet was a vast necklace, a throat protector, with hundreds of diamonds.

Flossie gasped.

Rose shrieked.

The ladies crowded forward, making little cries of delight. Devonny's stepmother removed the delicate cameo that Devonny was wearing, and carefully lifted Devonny's hair from her neck. Devonny felt as if her neck were being prepared for a sword, not a jewel.

"Granny's pebbles," said Lord Winden, enjoying the commotion. He and Florinda fastened it around Devonny's neck. Diamond ribbons hung from a diamond-encrusted band, utterly hideous and utterly magnificent.

It's my collar, thought Devonny. I'm his dog, he's my master.

"Oh, Devonny!" cried Rose, looking adoringly at Lord Winden. "In such a necklace, surely you will meet the Queen."

"The necklace is very old," said Lord Winden.

"Granny will tell you the history, but it's been around forever. Everybody's worn it."

"I shall have to have a daughter, then," said Devonny, "to wear it in her turn."

It was rude to refer to future daughters. A man wanted sons.

"No," said Lord Winden, denying the possibility of daughters. "You will pass Granny's pebbles on to our son's wife."

"Oh, dear Lord Winden," cried Florinda, good stepmother and excellent hostess, speeding away from Devonny's mention of girl babies, "I am in love with you myself. Devonny, darling, I see you wearing the family necklace, supervising the family castle! You will be welcome at every party. You will have dinner with the Prince of Wales!"

The Prince of Wales, thought Devonny, is a fat old lecher who drinks too much. "The American press," said Devonny, "does not think much of the current fad of marrying titles. There was an editorial in the *Tribune* that we American girls should seek noble hearts instead of noble names."

Lord Winden smiled engagingly. "I do not have a heart, my dear."

The others laughed at this funny little joke, but Devonny believed him.

He did not have a heart.

———

Tod was much taller than his little soccer team.

Six-year-old girls stared up at him, their little mouths open, their little clothes messed up, their little hairdos as windblown and confused as their expressions.

There had been no parent or adult willing to coach the six-year-old girls, and Tod's mother had informed her son that this would be good for him. He, Tod, would be their coach, and their role model.

The little girls were completely alien; he might as well have been coaching kangaroos or harp seals.

They did not have the concept of this game at all. They watched the ball now and then but did not get involved with it.

"Hit it with your shoelaces," said Tod patiently.

"Keep your eyes on the ball," he said constantly.

His little team couldn't do that. They had each other to watch, and Tod to watch, and the sky and the birds. They could not get a sense of the action. They were lost right there on their tiny playing field, inside their modified game.

He showed them how to hit the ball with his forehead, and his little girls quite reasonably fell down laughing at the sight of a big boy like Tod whacking a ball with his face.

But they loved him.

Tod had never been loved like that, the pure complete adoration of children for their teacher.

If he wanted them to bat balls off their ears, they would try. If he thought racing up and down a stretch of grass mattered, they would make it matter.

They were thrilled with the color of their team T-shirts (hot purple) but sadly disappointed with the name. "Laura's Fabric Shop?" said Elizabeth, who could read better than the others. "We thought we'd be Tod's Team!"

All his little girls had formal names: Elizabeth, Emily, Letitia, Judith, Constance. He thought they'd run harder if they had harder names, so he called them Liz, Em, Tish. "You're athletes now," he explained. "You're fighters. You're tough."

They were awed at this description of themselves, and by the end of practice were far more grass-stained than usual, and Tod told them he was proud.

"Devonny!" he yelled. "Keep your eyes on the ball."

Every little player ground to a halt. "We don't have a Devonny on the team, Tod," Tish told him gently.

Tod shivered, as if Devonny's hair had drifted across his face. "Right," he said. "I meant Liz."

I'm normal, Tod told himself, although he had never heard of a normal teenage boy agreeing to coach six-year-old girls' soccer. Time travel is abnormal. So it didn't happen.

Tod, who had never thought of texture in his life, who did not know the difference between velvet and denim, found himself remembering the texture of Devonny's gown. He had no word for that soft glossy stuff. He remembered her tears. For years, Tod had enjoyed making his sister cry—in fact, it was kind of a hobby of his, a successful hobby—but he felt pretty crummy remembering how easily he had made a strange girl cry. He remembered the curls, the strands of hair he had not touched but wanted to. The shock on her face when he left.

He had screwed up big-time. He should have stayed with her and helped.

This was a nauseating thought, and he got rid of it. The last thing he wanted was some romantic nonsense in his life.

"Em!" he bellowed. "Run the other direction!"

Emily eagerly ran the other direction, without remembering to try to take the ball with her. The ball lay alone and forgotten at the wrong end of the field.

Tod engaged his mind, putting it equally on soccer and designer water, leaving no spare brain cell for Devonny Stratton.

After dinner, so the gentlemen could enjoy their cigars and have an intelligent conversation, the ladies left the dining room.

Florinda, as hostess, led with Mrs. Van Stead, while Flossie, Rose and Devonny followed.

"We must discuss gowns," said Florinda as soon as they were all safely inside the parlor. "It's going to be so difficult, getting ready so quickly."

Rose, knowing she would be a bridesmaid, was wildly excited. "Ooooooh, this is so lovely! A grand, grand wedding and the attention of the world. And afterward, you shall live in England. People are so civilized there. Not like here."

"All Hugh-David wants is my money," said Devonny. Granny's pebbles had been returned to their leather case, but her throat felt dented from their weight.

"Then it's good you have lots of it," said Rose. "This is so unfair. Mother and I were husband hunting in Saratoga and we didn't encounter a single possibility. You didn't hunt for a moment, and up walks the most eligible creature to visit America in years!"

"I'm too young to husband-hunt," said Devonny.

"And I, too old," said Rose. "I am twenty-two, and I am getting frightened."

"There now," said Florinda, patting her. "You're a lovely lovely girl, and some fine young man is out there thinking of you even now."

But Rose was not lovely, and nobody was thinking of her, and they all knew it.

"We shall pair you with one of Lord Winden's eligible friends," said Florinda firmly. "That will be your task, Devonny. You must be sure that the groomsmen are unmarried and eager for brides. We will line up the wedding party accordingly."

"And my Flossie," said Mrs. Van Stead sharply, "must also be paired with a bachelor."

She suspects, thought Devonny. She knows Flossie is in love. But she can't know that the man is Johnny Annello. If she did know, we would be having a very different conversation. Well, I won't have true love, but Flossie must. "I think, Mrs. Van Stead," said Devonny archly, with much fluttering of eyes and tilting of cheek, "that I have seen Hugh-David's very dear friend Miles gazing upon Flossie. And all too boldly, I have seen Flossie gaze right back."

Mrs. Van Stead was delighted. Danger, for the moment, had passed.

Devonny's stepmother fussed at the neckline of Devonny's dress, tucking fabric down until all possible cleavage was visible. "We must enhance your wardrobe, Devonny," said Florinda. "Your gowns are childish. He will want you displayed." There was emphasis on the pronoun he, for the only person who mattered now was the he in Devonny's life.

Devonny gathered her courage. "What happens in a marriage, Florinda? What is the wedding night for?"

Flossie and Rose held their breath, and waited silently, just as desperate to know.

How uncomfortable the two older ladies looked.

Florinda gently returned the neckline to hide Devonny's figure again. "Well!" she said. "Do you remember the statues of nude men we saw when we traveled to Europe?"

"Yes."

"Do you remember that the men were shaped differently?"

Devonny remembered.

"Well, then. That's that. Now, Devonny, I believe I can convince Hiram that your dear mother must be part of the wedding planning. I see it as a way to get your mother quite a fine wardrobe. I can insist that she must be properly clothed for every event. Oh! A brilliant thought has come to me! Oh! Gather round!"

The ladies held hands in expectation.

"Devonny, I have seen the oil portrait of your dear mother in *her* wedding gown. We could remake it for your wedding! Of course it is completely out of style, but we would add hundreds of pearls! We would reset the sleeves to make them fashionable. And that way, you would be proud as you came down the aisle, and the hearts of your guests would be touched deeply, as you honored your dear mother."

The oil painting was in the attic in the city house. Facing the wall. Once Mama had been as slender and beautiful as Devonny, but abandonment and poverty had destroyed her.

"But," said Devonny, "I still don't know what happens when a man and a woman—"

"Hush. What happens is right. The man decides these things, and you obey."

"All right, but what does he decide?"

"Devonny, it is not ladylike to linger on these topics."

Before she could stop herself, Devonny said, "He has a mistress."

"Lord Winden?" said Rose. "How sophisticated!"

"It is not sophisticated!" said Devonny. "It is disgusting."

"You said you wanted to marry a man like your father," Rose said nastily.

I hate you, thought Devonny.

"It is all right for gentlemen to do that," said Mrs. Van Stead. "Do you know what they say in London? You may do anything you like, as long as you don't do it in the street and frighten the horses."

"That's fine for London," said Devonny, "but I'm packing Father's pistol, and if Winnie keeps seeing this woman, he's a dead man."

They laughed, as if Devonny had made a joke.

At last the ladies were summoned to rejoin the gentlemen, out on the glassed porch. A fire had been lit in the outdoor fireplace to take the chill off the evening.

Devonny and Flossie lingered until they were alone. Devonny whipped a letter out of her corset.

"Florinda almost found it when she played with my clothes. I was terrified!" They muffled their giggles while Flossie read.

*Dearest sweet Flossie,*

    *Now the fountain is complete. Now I have no reason to return to the Stratton estate. My heart aches. In front of my family, my crew and my friends, I laugh and talk. But my heart is in pain. I ache to be with you.*

    *We must name the day. Miss Stratton has promised to help.*

*All my love,*
*Gianni*

"Oh, Flossie, that's so beautiful!" whispered Devonny. "Does he mean the day you will elope? How will you get to him? Your mother suspects. She will not leave you unsupervised."

"I know!" whispered Flossie, glowing and sparkling with excitement. "Your wedding!" She clutched Devonny's arm. "In the excitement of the wedding, I will slip away. I will go with Johnny to City Hall and we will be married. Nobody will notice that I am gone until it is too late. It will be a double wedding, Devonny, but only you and I will know."

"What a beautiful plan!" breathed Devonny. "There will be a dozen bridesmaids, Flossie, and you will simply—"

Flossie's mother was upon them. "Give me that letter," hissed Mrs. Van Stead.

Flossie thrust it behind her, crumpling it, looking for a fire to throw it in. "No, Mama, please, it's private."

"Your father is outside the door, young lady. Would you like me to call him and have him see this letter?"

The threat of fathers was very great. Flossie bowed her head and handed the letter to her mother.

Her mother read it silently. "What a ridiculous name. Gianni. Why can't these people spell? Better yet, why can't they stay in Italy, where they belong?"

Flossie was weeping.

"This comes of allowing a girl to continue an education. I should never have permitted you to stay in school. It leads to false desires and weak mental behavior. You," said Mrs. Van Stead to her daughter, loathing and hatred in her voice, "will stay under my supervision."

She ripped the letter in many pieces. When it was reduced to confetti, she said, "We will not tell your father. It would destroy him."

"I'm sorry, Mama," whispered Flossie, trembling.

"Nor will I tell *your* father of *your* terrible behavior, Devonny," said Mrs. Van Stead. "I am shocked that you would cooperate with Flossie in her silliness. I am certainly glad you are marrying a strong man who will control you!"

She gripped each girl's arm and escorted them out like prisoners, all three pretending to be laughing and happy over nothing in particular, and nobody noticed a thing, because not noticing things was important in Society.

The evening passed, and when Devonny looked at her dear friend standing alone in the moonlight, Devonny knew that the fire in Flossie's heart simply burned stronger.

It came to Devonny that Flossie could still elope, on the very date they had thought of, using the very same plan. For Mrs. Van Stead had not shown the note to Mr. Van Stead, and Mrs. Van Stead could not know what "choose the date" meant.

The wedding that would mean prison for Devonny would be escape for Flossie Van Stead.

# FOUR

Police had blocked off the streets around Grace Church. The public lined the sidewalks early, for the best view of the wedding party, the famous, and the wealthy. There would be four hundred guests, each of whom must present the ivory vellum invitation. The police would let no one intrude upon the wedding.

Eleven bridesmaids, one maid of honor, the bride, the rector's wife, a florist, two seamstresses, and one stepmother filled the church parlor. The bridesmaids' gowns were old-fashioned, three shades of blush pink, with flounces and ruffles, the skirts so large that not an inch of floor was visible. Their delicate rose pink shoes were covered with seed pearls. Their flowers were white baskets filled with roses and stephanotis and ferns.

Day and night dressmakers had been at work. The crust of pearls added to her mother's wedding gown made the dress so heavy it took three bridesmaids to lift it over Devonny's head. When it was fastened on her body, she could not move. Her father would literally have to walk her down the aisle.

The stays had been laced very tightly. The bridesmaids cooed and ahhed at the amazing narrowness of her waist. This is my life, thought Devonny. Laced together by strangers, while a man decides where I walk.

"Oh, Devonny!" cried her friends. Gertrude and Flossie and Victoria, Ethel and Constanza and Ariel, Elizabeth and Rose and Muriel, Eunice and Charity crowded around to touch and gasp over the gown. "You are so beautiful," whispered Maud, her first cousin and maid of honor, though they were not close. "You make a perfect bride." Maud believed this: The gown was perfect, the face was perfect, and so the life would be perfect.

Harriett should have been maid of honor, but Harriett had died. Strat should have been best man, but Strat had vanished. And now Devonny Stratton, too, would vanish, across an ocean and into another name and life. Only Flossie would vanish by choice, and whether that choice was wise or terribly foolish, Devonny did not know.

The parlor was quite lovely: wallpaper of yellow roses, heavy church furniture, carved and mysterious. There were two doors: the door to the sanctuary, and the door to the side vestibule. From the vestibule, one could go outside, or into the parish house, the Sunday School rooms and the great hall.

Flossie's timing must be perfect. No one must notice her slip out of the parlor.

Devonny had seated Flossie's parents behind tall people, so they'd have a poor view of the aisle. Mrs. Van Stead was nearsighted and Devonny didn't think she could pick her own daughter out of the parade.

When the processional had ended, the girls would be lined up along the chancel, enormous gowns like a vast bouquet. If somebody were to count and find one bridesmaid missing, would anybody dream of interrupting the ceremony? No. They would assume the missing girl had fainted from excitement. Ladies did this.

Once Flossie got out of the church, there was no danger—the police, after all, were preventing people from entering, not from leaving. But Flossie had a long way to go, and Devonny would give her every minute she could. Devonny had insisted on an anthem by the boys' choir as well as a solo by the tenor. She was not satisfied with the reading of one psalm, but required three. She would repeat her vows slowly, with much heaving of her girlish breast.

Then would come the recessional, then lots of bustle and photographs, and waving at the public, and leaving for the reception. Very possibly, hours would pass before Mr. and Mrs. Van Stead knew that Flossie was not among the bridal party, and never had been.

The beautiful Gothic nave was filled with Society: matrons, businessmen, millionaires, elderly patrons of the arts. Men wore graceful swallowtail coats. Every lady had been given a corsage, every gentleman a boutonniere.

Not one member of Hugh-David's family was here.

Last night she had asked Hugh-David why not. Even though she was a purchased bride, was it not an event to celebrate?

Lord Winden had merely studied his hands, of which he was very proud. His hands were rather slight, not long or strong enough for work. Everything about Hugh-David was rather slight. "My mother will arrange family celebrations when we return home," he said. "There is every need for you to meet my people, but there is no need for my people to meet yours."

Every day on Devonny's breakfast tray had been a letter from Hugh-David. His letters were not affectionate; they were instructions. His plans, and how she would fit into them. They were un—love letters.

Through the parlor door came Devonny's mother. The first Mrs. Stratton's corsage was too heavy for her gown, and it lopped forward, dragging the dress with it. Though Florinda had arranged for a generous budget at the finest dress shop, poor Aurelia Stratton stood now in a new dress that did not quite fit and was not quite fashionable. She was twitching with anxiety, an apologetic smile darting in and out. Even Devonny could see why nobody invited Mother anywhere. A woman without a man was so completely nothing and nobody.

Last night the family had gathered to sign the contracts. Devonny, both her parents (no matter how many divorces he might have, Hiram's first wife was still Devonny's mother) and their lawyers, and Lord Winden and his lawyers met in the drawing room. Once the signatures were on the papers, the wedding could proceed.

It had been so strange to see Mama in the town house that had belonged to three other wives since. How Mama gaped at the magnificent rooms, as if more interested in the interior decorations that other wives had added or changed than in her own daughter. Oh, Mama! Devonny had thought, yearning to be alone with her parent.

Father had not permitted mother and daughter to talk alone.

Instead, he said *he* would talk to Devonny alone. She had been touched. This was, after all, the last time father and child would be together alone before she was a married woman. She had even smiled at him as they entered his study, as he shut the door behind him, thinking that now, at last, would come the words of encouragement, love and understanding.

"You're up to something, aren't you?" he said harshly. He jabbed the bowl of his lit pipe into her stomach. Father could not possibly know Flossie was going to elope right during the wedding. If he had figured that out, he would have gone to Mr. and Mrs. Van Stead.

"You want a scene," said her father. "You want to toss your pretty hair and refuse to sign the financial documents." He pinned her to the wall, the enormous shelf of his belly right against her. "If you do anything to delay, Devonny, if by one syllable you make Lord Winden feel unwanted, what is the punishment I explained you would receive?"

"I will never be wed, sir." A terrible cold isolated life, waiting in a back room, invited nowhere. No children, no love, no life, no hope. It made Lord Winden look desirable indeed.

"You will smile as you sign. You will kiss your fiancé on the cheek, and ask to hold his hand."

"Yes, Father."

And then he smiled. Devonny could never see that smile without remembering when Father read a letter from the asylum describing Strat's whippings. Father's smile had been so broad it lifted his entire mustache, like a shot rodent. "I have discovered the identity of the blackmailer."

What relief! The dreaded smile was not for her. "Who is it? Who is responsible? Is there time to stop him?"

Her father did not answer these questions. He said, "I need to know what you think I should do to this person."

Never had her father asked Devonny's opinion on anything. She was amazed and proud. But she had no answer. How could anybody be punished without publicity? How could the writer of that evil letter be sent to prison without a trial? Without reporters and scandal?

Was Father toying with her? Did he mean to call the wedding off? Did he, against all evidence, have her best interests at heart? Would there still be some way to back out of this ceremony? Send Lord Winden on his way? But no. Father would never tolerate the furor, the humiliation, the appalling laughter should the wedding be called off.

What an irony, to be safe from the threat and not be able to extricate herself from its consequences.

"I can destroy this person," said her father softly. "Total isolation, so that the writer of this letter sees neither friend nor foe once more. The writer will live for years, all in silence, all in solitude. No window.

No hope. Abandoned by all, hidden from all. Life reduced to waiting for a tray of cold food silently delivered by an unseen hand."

If I have to pay so high a price, thought Devonny, so should the evil blackmailer. "Yes, Father! Do that!"

And her father had smiled his terrible rat-and-mongrel-eating smile, and she knew that somehow, in some dreadful way, she had been tricked. But into what? For what?

And now . . . the wedding.

The church was laced with flowers: ropes of flowers, towers of flowers. The organ played magnificently. The boys' choir, robed in scarlet, sang sweetly. But the bride's heart sank.

"You look lovely, Mama," she said, although it was not true. Her mother flinched as if struck and turned away. Poor Mama!

Devonny's father entered.

The presence of a man changed the girls. Eyes dropped and voices lowered. Women might prepare for a great event, but a man would control it.

"Aurelia," said her father sharply to her mother.

"Yes, Hiram."

"The groomsman will seat you now."

"Yes, Hiram."

The bride and her mother silently touched cheeks, and then the first Mrs. Stratton took the arm of the head usher. She would traverse the aisle to Handel's *Water Music,* stately but joyful. Devonny hoped her mother could think of this as a happy event.

Devonny said, "A kiss, dear Flossie."

There was a shifting of gowns, a pressing up against one another, to give Flossie room to reach Devonny. She and Flossie touched cheeks. Her own was blazing hot. The pink of her complexion would please the guests. Flossie's cheek was cold and afraid. Slowly the girls released each other and stepped back. Would they see each other again in this life? Would their husbands permit it?

The bridesmaids lined up. There was not room to form a straight line, so they curled among each other, giggling and excited.

Maud, as maid of honor, tucked the veil over Devonny's face, careful to crush none of the flowers in Devonny's hair arrangement.

It was safe behind the veil. No one could see into her eyes and know what she felt, or what she and Flossie had planned.

Devonny had a surprising memory of the months in California, when she had flirted with Randal. She remembered the sun, how it never failed; the boys, how relaxed and full of laughter. In California, there was a sense of time, time to do whatever came up, time to laugh and talk and be.

I am out of time, thought Devonny.

Tod Lockwood did not normally read books. He obeyed his teachers and turned in his assignments, and this did mean reading. Whole pages. Now and then a complete book. His sister had given him a book for a good-bye present when she left for Norway. "You are boring, Tod. You need to widen your horizons. So I've bought you a travel guide." Tod hadn't even glanced at the title. He was just grateful that a sister who understood him so poorly was leaving the country.

Months later, he happened upon the book, and here it was a travel guide to *The World's Most Dangerous Places*. Tod was hooked. So far he'd studied up on visiting Chechnya (where everybody was busy slaughtering each other) and Algeria (where wacko fundamentalists and war veterans liked to cut throats), and now he was deep into Colombia (a must-see, explained the author, for anybody planning a vacation in hell).

He found himself deeply restless, as if he *could* have gone to all those dangerous places, but had opted to stay home.

He kept walking away from the book, as if from his failed self, and walking back to stare at the title.

He had traveled to a dangerous place, and by a dangerous route. And what had he done in the presence of danger? He had pretended it wasn't happening. Brushed off the girl who needed him; him specifically; not just anybody! Him, Annie's brother!

He felt loose inside, as if his heart and lungs and guts were going their own way, leaving him to gasp and writhe.

He felt Devonny's fear, and heard his own stupid words. Over and over he saw himself stepping away from her, going back to his dumb designer water when he was needed in another world.


Her father glowed with pride. A man must create a strong son and a beautiful daughter. Well, the strong son had been a bad son, and now was either a missing son or a dead son, but Devonny had turned out to be a beautiful and obedient daughter.

He did not embrace her. She could not recall ever being hugged by her father. He jutted his elbow toward her, and she tucked her gloved hand around his arm and surrendered to her fate.

The music ceased. The preludes were over; now it remained only to move the bridal party to the altar.

There was a moment of total expectant silence.

Nobody had seen the wedding gown. Most guests had not seen the groom, and a view of a titled Englishman was always delightful. Now, in this silence, the rector and Hugh-David would be emerging from the sacristy to wait for Devonny near the altar.

In the curving bridesmaid line, Flossie was closest

to the side door and the cloakroom. Devonny must permit no one to see Flossie step back into the vestibule. "Oh, Father," she said, looking up at his big drooping walrus mustache, his grossly fat neck, as wedged into its starched collar as she was into her corset. Do I love my father? she thought. I don't think so. How could anybody love him? And yet—I want to please him. I want to have a family full of love. "How I wish Strat were here," she said. "I miss him so."

He softened. (Hiram Stratton in a soft moment!) "I, too, Devonny. Now be my brave girl. This is best for all of us."

The trumpets began. Their climbing chords of celebration filled the great stone chamber, and then were joined by the massive organ. Even Devonny was thrilled. The stone lace of Grace Church, the chilly beauty of its gothic peaks and arches, spoke to her soul.

The first bridesmaid, Muriel, moved out of the parlor and down the great aisle. She was trembling. Her basket of flowers quivered. The guests turned to stare, but they did not stand. They would stand only for Devonny.

Esther, the second bridesmaid, followed.

Then Constanza, the third.

Now the girls could straighten their line, while the seamstresses knelt to fluff crinolines and tug at hems.

No one looked at anything except the aisle down which she would walk.

Devonny felt the motion of Flossie leaving.

She squeezed her father's arm to keep his attention on her, and to her amazement, he patted her hand, as if he loved her.

Perhaps he does, she thought. Perhaps Hugh-David will too, one day, and perhaps I will love them. I must believe that.

The fourth bridesmaid took her first step, and at the same moment, the side door gently closed.

Devonny Aurelia Victoria Stratton prayed for the future of Mrs. Gianni Annello.

The fifth bridesmaid.

The sixth.

Flossie must have her coat on by now, the faded shapeless one she had stashed in the back hall. Her bouquet would be tossed on a shelf, pins yanked from her hair, ribbons stuffed in her pocket, big old scarf tied over her head. She wouldn't waste time buttoning the coat, just pull it around herself, and surely by now she was out of the church and among the crowd.

Her father said casually, "By the way, in the morning I shall begin the punishment of the writer of that letter."

How unfair of Father, how crude, to mention the blackmail now!

"Your mother wrote that letter," said her father,

smiling. His big yellow teeth moved like a horse grinding over its bit. "She thought if you were married to a titled Englishman, you would send for her; she would go to live in England, and have a wonderful life after all, and see the Queen, and have fine clothing again."

The seventh bridesmaid left.

"But she is mistaken," said Hiram Stratton. "She will be sealed in the attic. I expect she will survive for two or three decades. With no sun, no air, no visits, no sounds, no friends, no daughter. But food, of course. I want to sustain life, so that she may continue to suffer."

The eighth bridesmaid.

Devonny swayed, and her father's ham-sized hand supported her. "No one crosses me," he said softly. "I am glad that you agreed on the punishment."

The ninth bridesmaid.

"Mother wrote the letter?" whispered Devonny. But yes, she could see it now. The handwriting was Mother's, and the beautiful paper. Oh, the desperation! the poverty! the joylessness! that had made this seem rational to Mama. Mama, in the dark shabby cold house in Brooklyn, whispering to herself, scratching out a letter, planning her new life, believing it would come true.

The tenth bridesmaid.

"No, Father," she breathed through the veil, standing on tiptoe to get close to his ear. "Let Mother go. It doesn't matter. I am proud to be wed as you choose. I shall be the best of wives. I promise that I shall do exactly as I am told, forever. I shall always behave! Please do not punish Mama!"

"Your mother made her choices and she will suffer her consequences."

"She didn't choose to be divorced, Father! She didn't choose to live in poverty."

The rector's wife and the florist and the seamstresses closed in on them. "So sweet," said the rector's wife, patting Devonny's bare shoulder, "to see you and your dear papa sharing these last minutes."

The flower girls—Ethel's three-year-old twins, gold hair in ringlets—were readied. They carried baskets of rose petals to strew so that Devonny would walk on flowers. The little girls were giggling and afraid and thrilled.

Oh, Strat! Come save me! Oh, somebody! Please save me! Save Mama, save me from knowing what my own mother did, save me from this marriage, don't let me know the truth about my parents, don't let me find out what marriage is from this man who can't even be bothered to invite anybody, please please save me.

"Here we are!" beamed the rector's wife. "Last in line!"

I am last in line, thought Devonny. I am quite literally last in line. Everyone else comes ahead of me.

Lord Hugh-David Winden loved clothing, and had chosen his as carefully as any woman in the church. Gordon and Miles stood with him, while the ushers (people Hiram Stratton knew; nobody who mattered) formed a long swallow-tailed row behind them.

The flowers that filled the great sanctuary had been sped by train from the American South. How delightful to know that he, too, would be able to afford trainloads of hothouse flowers.

He felt a surprising surge of emotion as the bridesmaids appeared. How slowly they approached, trumpet music their only escort. The girls were beautiful, even the plain ones.

Devonny. A strange but beautiful name, just as American girls were strange but beautiful.

Americans believed they could create themselves. Always the singing lesson, the dancing lesson, the drawing lesson. Always studying foreign languages and history. If you tried hard enough, said the American girl, you could achieve anything. It was a matter of will.

Devonny had plenty of will.

He was eager to see how Devonny managed his

mother. Lord Winden's mother was overwhelming, especially to Lord Winden. A wife like Devonny might actually be an ally; together, he and his new wife might . . . No. These things rarely happened. The marriages he knew were full of trauma. Men and wives led separate lives.

He counted bridesmaids.

To his amazement, Hugh-David could hardly wait to see his bride. What will the gown look like? he thought. Will she be the vision I'm expecting? Will she be hidden by a veil? Will she be weeping? Will she smile?

Gordon whispered in his ear. "She's so embarrassingly American, Hugh. You shall have to perform radical surgery on her."

Hugh-David allowed a slight smile to decorate his formal expression. Gordon had witnessed Devonny beating him at tennis, riding her bicycle with a split skirt, and even, when she fell off the bike, jumping up in disgust and shrieking a swear word. Gordon had been horrified and amused, muttering that Hugh-David would have to be very careful, lest the girl turn into her father: fat, stomping and vulgar. But Hugh-David had found her immensely attractive. Not ladylike. But attractive.

He knew he had been a tiny bit mean to Devonny, but it was essential, with a headstrong young girl, to be sure she knew whose world she was entering. His.

It was his hunt, his shoot, his yacht, his party, his estate.

He would be kind to her during the voyage, but he would structure their lives so that she learned to obey.

One bridesmaid to go.

Then the flower girls.

Then the bride. His bride. His new property.

In the space where pink ruffled skirts and white baskets of flowers had been, Devonny began to see something very odd.

An angel was joining them.

Devonny could see the angel quite clearly, and just as the Bible said, the angel was a beautiful man.

He did not have flesh, just form. She could make out his outlines, but not his body. He was kneeling, which seemed fine for an angel.

Her father was not looking.

Devonny whispered to the angel, "Am I to die? Is that to be my fate?"

Now the angel did not look like an angel at all, but more like a devil, strangely familiar. Devonny narrowed her eyes, trying to focus on him.

Her father said, "Come, Devonny."

She could not move. He put his large heavy hand on her waist, half circling it, and, with the church ladies, launched her forward. The gown followed, the train weighing so much it was like towing furniture.

The angel stood up.

It was no angel. It was Tod Lockwood.

Her father continued to walk, in the slow awkward shift of body they called "the hesitation step." His great weight pulled her along.

Tod had come for her, as his sister, Annie, had once come for Strat.

Flossie yanked the crinoline down, stepped out of it, smashed the enormous stiff undergarment beneath her feet and crammed it behind some old pew, pulled silk and ribbons out of her hair and chucked them into the umbrella stand. Flinging her arms into her old coat, she turned the circular handle of the old wooden door and eased herself out onto the street.

This was the back of the church; the crowds were massed out front for the best view. If people turned, all they would see was a woman in an ill-fitting coat, tying an old scarf over her messy hair. Flossie walked away. The bridesmaid skirt was a little too long, and she kept catching her slippers on it. Around the corner, on a park bench, she sat down to rip the lowest ruffle right off. There. Now she wouldn't fall.

She stuffed the pink satin strip into a pocket of the coat and ran on. The delicate slippers were not designed for pavement, and began to tear apart in only a few blocks.

The sky was not yet winter gray, but still autumn blue. The sun was thin but friendly, and the city seemed buoyant and happy to Flossie. She jumped puddles and broken sidewalk slates. She circled peddlers and cabbies and shoppers and nannies.

Laughter bubbled in her throat and smiles danced on her face. She, Florence Elizabeth Ruth Van Stead, was going to become Mrs. Gianni Annello.

By now, the wedding procession would be finished. Her mother and father, neatly seated in their pew, her father's top hat on his lap, her mother's egret feathers towering above anybody else's, would be proudly turning to see their daughter.

But between Rose and Eunice there would be no Flossie.

They must have changed the order, her mother would think. Flossie will be next.

But instead, the flower girls would come.

How on earth did I miss her? Mother would wonder, trying to discern the girls already near the altar. Mother would not dream of disfiguring her face with spectacles, and would not be able to see. Father, though he would be confused, would not remark on it, for weddings were the stuff of females, and he would just assume he had misunderstood.

The ceremony would last over an hour because of all the music and scripture Devonny had added. By that time, Flossie and Johnny would have reached City Hall. By the time Devonny and her groom finished with the receiving line, why, Flossie and Johnny might have said their *own* marriage vows!

She was hugging herself with joy. She could feel the shape of Johnny inside her arms. She could hardly wait to see his beautiful smile, hear his exuberant laugh.

She reached Washington Square and rushed to the elm under which they had agreed to meet.

No Johnny was there.

Benches lined the park. Oak and ash and plane trees were bare now, and the fallen leaves swirled about her ankles. Flossie walked carefully, neatly, not letting herself think about it, past every bench sitter. She smiled at the pretty little dogs on leashes and the sweet children in perambulators.

No Johnny.

The magnificent new arch, in honor of George Washington, made a brilliant gateway. She walked calmly to the arch, and around it, and through it, but Johnny was nowhere to be seen.

She stood beside the statue of Garibaldi, presented by the Italians of New York, but her own personal Italian was not there.

She found a bench. She sat on the very edge, ready to leap into the air at the first sight of him.

The minutes passed.
The sun moved down in the sky.
Johnny Annello did not come.

Hiram Stratton liked the idea of a title in the family. England ruled the world, and Parliament was her voice. And what a world England was! India and Hong Kong and Australia and Kenya . . .

His daughter would enter that world; her money would give that man more power; Hiram's grandchildren would inherit everything: the Stratton millions, the Winden estates, the power of the British Empire!

Devonny had wanted to marry a man who would accomplish something. With my money, my dear, thought Hiram Stratton, patting her little gloved hand as he studied the famous faces along the church aisle, perhaps he will. After all, somebody is going to have to rule India. Why not Winden?

Ruling an entire country was an attractive thought. Hiram thought he would practice saying India the way the British pronounced it: Innn-jah!

A moment ago, they had been moving forward, but now they stopped. Hiram Stratton assumed the flower girls were slow, and he thought nothing of it. The church pleased him: filled with people come to admire his daughter's beauty and his daughter's titled catch. Wives would stare at Lord Winden and be jealous, because this great catch had gone to somebody else's daughter. Husbands would stare at Devonny and wish they were young again.

There was nothing quite so wonderful as Society feeling jealous of you.

He was oddly impressed by his ex-wife's strategy. Aurelia had done an excellent job. He hated to admit how readily he had been conned into action he had not planned. The woman had almost gotten away with it. But Aurelia had given him two great gifts: the gift of this wedding and glorious future . . . and the gift of her punishment.

He felt a frisson of pleasure at the thought of her life to come.

He planned her next few hours. The wedding, of course, would be a triumph. Aurelia, unknowing of her fate, would be escorted back to the seashore mansion, while Devonny and her groom left for their journey on one of the great cross-Atlantic ships. Devonny would quickly forget her mama. And he, Hiram Stratton, who forgot nothing, ever, would enjoy watching the carpenters nail boards over the windows, while Aurelia chose which blanket to keep with her in the unheated attic.

Hiram felt a strange cold tug, as if some fool had opened a door to winter and let in a vicious wind.

He turned, and his face hurt slightly, icy in spite of the brushy thick beard and draping mustache. He put his hand up as if to wipe away snow, and in doing so, he realized that Devonny's arm was not resting on his, and that Devonny—

—that Devonny—

*Devonny!*


Tod's university sweatshirt was a size extra large, although Tod himself was medium. It hung to his hips, and the cuffs went past his fingertips. His sneakers were his old ones, without decent laces, so they hung open like dogs' mouths. His baseball cap was on backward, and his hair, which badly needed a trim, stuck out irregularly along the edges. His braces had broken during the week but Tod had not been in the mood to see the orthodontist, so he'd just smudged on that gummy wax the dentist gave you to cover rough braces edges.

Time was ice, was zero.

His skin, his teeth, his fingers, his gut hurt from the cold. He closed his eyes, but the brutal wind burned through his lids. He felt like a skier going down an advanced slope in Canada in February wearing only a T-shirt. His skin would come off, he would die or be hospitalized.

Tod tried to come to grips with his sister's courage, doing this willingly, but the cold and wind and speed were too terrible. He could only wait it out. He was Time's property.

He had agreed to come, but he had expected to run the show.

He had a sense of landing, and a sense that he could refuse to let his body arrive completely, and a sense that even for one who wanted to travel to dangerous places, this was not wise. He could not find a grip, or a purpose, just cold and fear. His stretching hand found Devonny's, and he seized it, and flung himself back the way he had come.


In their pew, Mr. and Mrs. Van Stead smiled at one another.

How well they had handled the potential disaster with the Italian boy! Luckily, a loyal servant had showed them yet another of those foolish letters. The ridiculous girl had actually intended to *marry* the stonecutter! It was revolting, but whatever silly little plan their daughter had cooked up would not work now.

Mr. Van Stead had had the boy picked up. Gianni Annello was on his way back to Italy.

The captain of the cargo ship had promised to keep him locked up until the ship was safely out to sea, and that took care of that.

Scandal had been averted. And if Flossie's heart was broken—well, headstrong young girls needed to be broken before marriage, like colts.

Mrs. Van Stead could not see Flossie among the

pink blurs at the front, but she hoped that Gordon or Miles was looking at her fondly. Hoped Gordon or Miles was sufficiently broke to want Flossie, because it was certainly necessary to get Flossie married instantly. Why, the girl's behavior implied a low-class, animal, physical attraction to that boy!

Rearing girls was so difficult, and so unrewarding.

Hiram Stratton said thickly, "Where is my daughter?"

The church ladies stared at him, looking wildly around, as if Devonny were a teacup that must be sitting on a shelf somewhere.

The flower girls went down the aisle, strewing their rose petals. The trumpet music ceased. There was a pause in which everybody straightened, for this was the one time in a lady's life in which she was important: this short walk, in this long gown.

But there was no bride.

# FIVE

❧

*T*he guests were having a wonderful time.

*No bride!*

They were thoroughly enjoying the humiliation of the groom; most eager to witness the fury of the father. Some of the guests stood on the velvet-cushioned pews for a better view.

The bridesmaids could do nothing but stand in their semicircle, clinging to their baskets.

The groom remained calm. How British! He stood as coolly as if this were merely a problem with the gown, a torn hem perhaps, and any moment his bride would glide into his arms.

How could Devonny complain about securing a catch like this? thought Constanza. The man is handsome, courteous and needs her money. There's nothing quite so nice in a marriage as being needed.

Then came a thought so hideous and exciting that

Constanza had to share it with Rose. "What if Devonny has jilted him?"

"She wouldn't dare," whispered Rose without moving her lips. "Leave the man standing at the altar? In front of everybody? With a crowd of hundreds outside to know about it, and a dozen reporters to put it in every paper?"

"Nobody would forgive her," added Eunice, who hoped it was a jilting. She had always wanted to witness such a thing, and here she was, only a few feet from the groom. Such a handsome fellow. Perhaps—

No. If an American jilted him, he would go back across the Atlantic in the morning and never associate with Americans again. In fact, if Devonny jilted Lord Winden, it would ruin everybody's chance of grabbing a title. Eunice became angry at Devonny. What a wretched thing to do to the rest of them! Devonny was so selfish.

"Where is Flossie?" Eunice whispered to Constanza.

"Between you and Elizabeth," whispered Constanza, irritated. Wasn't this delay awkward enough without Eunice being a fool?

Constanza looked up and down the semicircle to be sure she was correct that Flossie stood between Eunice and Elizabeth.

There was no Flossie.

Constanza studied the entire line. Flossie was not among them. How very peculiar. Had Flossie felt too faint to march in? Or had Flossie joined the search for Devonny?

From the back came a huge bellow, a voice that seemed too large even for the large body of Hiram Stratton. "My daughter! My daughter has been kidnapped! I was warned! But I did not take it seriously! My daughter has been kidnapped!"

The most difficult thing Hugh-David Winden had ever done was to walk back down that aisle . . . without a bride. He smiled courteously at the guests, ignored their hot gossipy eyes, said nothing to the barbed taunts they meant him to overhear. He made it out of the sanctuary and into the parlor, where Hiram Stratton was shouting to the police. "A man snatched her. Right from my arms!"

"Are you sure she didn't just leave?" said a policeman sternly. "Jilting a man has been done, sir. Done a lot more than kidnapping."

Hugh-David wondered which he would prefer. To be publicly humiliated—a man so undesirable that a lady had to flee the church rather than be united with him—or to have Devonny's life in jeopardy.

"It's true!" cried the florist. "She was here and then she wasn't!"

"I saw him!" shouted Hiram. "It was kidnapping!"

He was red in the face, strangled by his collar and his fury. "He took my daughter's arm and snatched her! I should have hired more police! Why didn't you stop this heinous event?"

Miles and Gordon had followed Lord Winden out of the church. Now Miles pressed up against Hugh-David. "We must leave," he whispered. "I knew this Stratton fellow was so abominable only the worst could happen."

Miles and Gordon would take this humiliation home with them. They'd dine out on the story for years. How amused his mother and brothers and cousins would be. It hardly bore thinking of.

"No money is worth this, Hugh," said Gordon. "Cut your losses and quit."

Devonny was a bet, and I lost, thought Hugh-David. Time to fold.

The bridesmaids had joined them, sobbing and crying out, their huge gowns rustling, the thorns from their roses poking and stabbing. "Do you really mean it?" came their cries. "A threat against Devonny? How could you not have told us? How could you let this happen, Mr. Stratton?"

In the midst of Hugh-David's anger and humiliation came a splinter of fear. The girls were genuinely afraid for Devonny. If she were jilting me, he thought, she would have confided in one of them. Or in all of them. But she did not.

The police rushed senselessly around the church, as if a bride in a flowing white gown had slid behind a pillar or was resting in the chapel.

Hiram Stratton could not describe the kidnapper or the kidnapper's clothing. He could not explain how his daughter had been taken from him without a fight.

He insisted the kidnapper was alone. But how could one man, wondered Hugh-David, no matter how strong and determined, lift a bride whose gown was so heavy the bride herself could not move? The Devonny who had beaten him in golf and tennis, who had ridden a horse and a bike, who had talked back and argued—wouldn't this Devonny have resisted? Surely at least she would have dropped her flowers; she would have screamed.

Hiram Stratton was having a tantrum, pounding a heavy carved oak chair on the stone floor.

It's Hiram Stratton who demanded speed, thought Hugh-David. Hiram Stratton who set the wedding date for one month from my request for Devonny's hand. I was in no rush. After all, my bills have not been paid in months, some of them not in years. Let my creditors wait longer, I don't care.

Is it Hiram who now does not want it? Could Hiram Stratton himself have arranged a kidnapping? But to what end? No man wants scandal involving his daughter. And if he wanted to call off the wedding, he would never have done it in front of his own guests.

The police found nobody outside the church who had seen the bride. A dress described as vast, ornate and glittering? A thousand onlookers could not have missed Devonny's exit.

They began a grim search of cellar and belfry, back stairs and offices, classrooms and kitchens. Plenty of places to drag a girl—perhaps smothered by a drug, perhaps strangled by a wicked hand—and plenty of places to have a carriage waiting.

Hugh-David thought of what could happen to a beautiful sixteen-year-old girl in the hands of thugs.

"Kidnapping!" exclaimed Gordon. "It's so American, so vulgar. You cannot have this scandal attached to your name."

"It is not attached to my name," said Hugh-David. "It is attached to Miss Stratton's." She would be ruined. No one would marry a girl who might have been raped. No one. Including Hugh-David.

Hugh-David found himself comforting the mother, the real mother, the first Mrs. Stratton. The poor thing was sobbing uncontrollably. "What will become of me now?" she said over and over.

What will become of *you*? thought Hugh-David, shocked. How could the woman think of herself instead of her daughter?

Gordon muttered, "Come, Hugh. It is unthinkable that you should have anything more to do with this Stratton crowd."

But they had forgotten Hiram Stratton, and his great bulk, and temper, and power.

"There is no crowd of Strattons," said Hiram. "There is one Stratton, and I am he." He smiled a terrible smile, his lips stretched like cords. In his jowls a muscle twitched, making his beard jump. "And you, Hugh-David Winden, will stay. My innocent name is at stake."

*Your* name? Hugh-David was stunned, for he had thought Devonny surrounded by love. But Devonny's father and mother had no more regard for Devonny than Hugh-David's father and mother had for him.

"Really, sir!" said Gordon coldly to Mr. Stratton. "There is no need to behave like a ruffian on a frontier."

Hugh-David remembered himself in the garden at the mansion by the sea, playing games with her—this very young girl about to become his wife—and saying to her, "I do not have a heart, my dear."

She is alone and terrified in the hands of evil, thought Hugh-David, *and knows better than to expect anything from me.*

The man who had Devonny was the most shocked of all. He had not had a master plan; if he had, it would not have included bringing Devonny into his time, wearing a dress the size of a school bus, carrying enough flowers for two funerals, and sobbing from behind a veil.

"My mother!" she cried. "How will I save my mother? She will be held responsible! Father will keep her alive in the attic for decades! She will suffer so! Where is this? Where are we? Strat must be here! Do you have Strat? He will know what to do, you don't know anything! Why are you wearing a shirt with a hog on it?"

Tod was offended. He had a large collection of college team sweatshirts, and razorback hogs were the best. She had just insulted his favorite sweatshirt. "I told you before, I don't have Strat!" he yelled back.

"Then take me home!"

"How am I supposed to do that? Throw you at the pump handle? Toss you in the sea? What are you doing in that ridiculous dress? I can't even fit you through the car door."

"You came to rescue me, now rescue me!"

"What am I supposed to do with you?" he yelled.

"You're supposed to help me find my brother!"

He stopped yelling because he was giving himself a sore throat, but also because runners were approaching. It was too late in the year for sunbathing or sailing, but runners never knew when to quit.

To his disgust, Tod knew the runners: four girls in his high school who were on the varsity basketball team and thought they were perfect. They were wearing designer spandex, tighter than skin, and designer sneakers, and designer sweatbands, and as they ran up to him, laughing hysterically at the sight of Devonny in her wedding gown, they came to a halt but continued running in place.

"What is *this*?" shrieked Tory, giggling at Devonny.

"What a hoot!" said Jill, poking at the skirt, which appeared to be covered in jewels. Tod could not imagine how they got jewelry to stick to the skirt. There had to be a million little pearls on there.

Tod hated being laughed at. And to think he had worried about her and let himself get involved! Women!

"This is Annie's friend, Devonny," said Tod with dignity, "and we are participating in a contest. You guys are ruining it for us. After all we've gone through, now we're going to lose! Get out of the picture."

"Are you being filmed?" said Tory, horrified that she might be ruining a movie.

"Of course we're being filmed! Do you think she would dress like this and yell at me like this for any other reason? Beat it!" yelled Tod. "You're supposed to be runners. Run."

The girls were smart enough to see there were no cameras around, no film crews. But there had to be, or why would this woman be dressed so weird? Embarrassed and uncertain, they jogged out of range of whatever was going on.

"Get in the car, Devonny," Tod muttered. He could hardly budge her. The gown weighed more than all his gallons of water. He shoved her toward his ancient station wagon. Nobody drove station wagons anymore; his parents had bought the thing for Annie, and this year Tod inherited it. It was immense and tanklike. Mr. and Mrs. Lockwood said if a car accident happened, the other guy would be squished like a tuna fish can, while Annie or Tod would drive away with nothing more than a scratch on the bumper.

But it was impossible to stuff Devonny in. First of all, she would not cooperate, and second of all, her dress wouldn't crumple up enough. "That dress has gotta go." He yanked a pair of blue jeans from the backseat (Tod did not believe in doing laundry; he just stored used clothing wherever he might need it), snatched up a T-shirt he used to clean the windshield, and thrust them in her face. "Wear these. We gotta look normal. I gotta think of something to do with you."

She had taken off her veil, at least, and now turned her back to him. "You'll have to unbutton me."

Fifty-six teeny-weeny little buttons he could hardly get his fingers around. Tod could not believe this was happening to him. He refused to turn around to see how the runners were behaving.

Underneath the huge gown she had another gown, satiny, with a definite resemblance to something from the inner pages of the Victoria's Secret catalog. Whoa, thought Tod. Devonny tried to stuff the gown down into the jeans.

"Zipper goes in front," said Tod. "Gimme the bottom dress, you can't wear that either. I'm not looking, I'm busy folding up your dresses. Put on this T-shirt."

Devonny was facing the strange, bounding females in that hideous clothing, which clung to their very outlines. Did they think they were mermaids? Men were not supposed to know what girls looked like. It made her so uncomfortable to think of Tod viewing these things.

Now he wanted her to take off her undergarments! Summoning her courage, Devonny peeled them off. Tod had lied and was looking after all. *"What is that thing?"* he said, horrified.

How could he be horrified by a perfectly sensible corset and not even notice a woman wearing a purple skin? But then she remembered that Annie had not known what a corset was either. Annie had had on the strangest little connected flowery cups instead. Devonny pulled the white shirt on. It was not clean. She could not believe she was wearing a shirt with filth on it.

"I can't wear so little clothing," she whispered,

starting to cry. Tod peeled off his own shirt—a bizarre heavy thing without a front or back opening—and yanked it down over her head.

Devonny had certainly never imagined the moment would come when she would wear a picture of a pig on her body. But the long heavy sleeves felt good, sort of fleecy, and she felt safer inside it.

Tod crammed the entire wedding gown into the back of his motor car, and she shuddered, thinking how it might rip or acquire a stain, and then she remembered that she did not care about this gown, nor the occasion for which she had worn it.

"Get in front," he ordered her, but she could not locate the door, and Tod had to stuff her in and then encircle her with straps to hold her down. "I won't go anywhere," she assured him.

"I can't believe this is happening to me," he said. He twisted a key near his lap and the vehicle roared. Devonny screamed. "It's okay," he shouted, "I just need a new muffler. Not to worry."

The vehicle leaped away. Roaring, it flew down roads that did not exist on Devonny's estate. And yet she was on her own estate, her summer cottage, even though her wedding had been in New York City. How had this happened? How had Tod come for her, all the while keeping his feet on the ground here? She did not feel rescued. She felt as if things were a hundred times worse.

She had to believe that Strat was waiting for her; that wherever Tod was taking her was a place where Strat had been, and would be again, and Strat would know what to do.

Tod's motorcar faced right at other vehicles, not one of which had the same shape or color, but all of which roared and rushed and glittered. He did not smash any of them, but it was not for lack of trying.

She covered her eyes and tried not to sob. What have I done? thought Devonny. How can I undo it?

She peeked between her fingers. They were leaving her estate and hurtling at incredible speed toward the village. She recognized a building here and there, but was badly shaken by the number of houses. Not an inch of farm or meadow. Houses, houses, houses.

"Do you have to go so fast?" she whispered.

"We're crawling. We're doing forty."

"I'm going to throw up," said Devonny.

"Don't even think about it," said Tod. "Bad enough I have to take the dog to the vet's — I'm not cleaning up after you!"

"You are a hateful rude unpleasant mean person."

"You got it," said Tod. "And now we have to think of an explanation to give my mother and father for why a hateful rude unpleasant mean guy like me is rescuing you."

"I don't call this a rescue," said Devonny.

"You got out of the wedding, didn't you?"

She began sobbing. "But my father will never forgive me! And he will take it out on my mother! It will all be my fault, even though I didn't mean any of it to happen. And no man will ever marry me now. Not after leaving my groom at the altar!"

"He was standing there?" said Tod, looking happy. "Cool. I wonder what they're doing. Wonder how he's handling it? Is he the kind of guy who can deal?"

Devonny struggled with Tod's vocabulary. She could not imagine Hugh-David doing anything but vanishing. A ship, a horse, a hotel—he would go, wiping Devonny from his thoughts the way his manservant wiped mud from his shoes.

"The problem is what to do next," said Tod. "We have to think of a good lie for Mom and Dad."

"It's wrong to lie to your parents," Devonny told him.

"Dev, my parents will not deal well with the truth. I know—you're an exchange student. You're from England. Can you do a British accent? Your host family didn't work out, you've gotta have a place to stay for a few days, and I volunteered—since my sister's on an exchange, it seemed only fair. Let's hear your British accent. Talk for me."

Devonny had practiced a British accent, but it embarrassed her. It was beautiful when the English spoke, but she just sounded pathetic. She mustered her courage and said in her most British voice, imitating the plummy elegant sounds of Hugh-David, "How terribly kind of you, Mrs. Lockwood, to welcome me into your home in my hour of need. Your son is a hero in my eyes."

"That's pouring it on a little thick," said Tod. "They know I'm not a hero, and I don't want anybody to think I like you or anything."

Devonny stopped worrying about their speed. In an even more British accent, she said, "How terribly kind of you, Mrs. Lockwood, to allow me to visit. My sympathies about your son. It must be difficult to live with such a cad."

Tod howled with laughter. "They'll love it, Dev. It's perfect."

The vehicle stopped in front of a strange-looking house, sharp angles with windows in the wrong places. The top piece of house was larger than the bottom piece of house, as if it had arrived at the wrong place. Tod drove straight toward two large wooden squares as if he meant to drive right into the building—and then he touched a button on the lid of his vehicle, the building opened and he *did* drive in.

Rusting containers and bent tools hung on the stable walls. Boxes of empty jars and cans stood next to a bicycle with a twisted wheel.

Tod slid out of his seat and strode into the house.

I must have hope, Devonny told herself. I am like a

Pilgrim from the Old World sailing with blind hope across the ocean. I, however, sailed across Time. Its shores are unknown to me, even as they were unknown to the pioneers. I must believe that Tod will reach my brother, and my brother will know what to do.

Devonny struggled with the black straps he had locked around her. They would not come away. She pulled at the one around her waist but it held tightly. She could not release herself. Dust and dark closed in on her.

Flossie was pressed up against the side of a brick building, furtively staring at the little park where she had expected Johnny to be. She had torn the frail lace of her gloves scraping them back and forth against the bricks. She had pulled her coat so tight against cold and fear that the seams were ripping.

She had sacrificed all . . . and Johnny was not here.

The grief that swept over her was hot. Shame was a fever.

She remembered every syllable Johnny had ever said in her presence. His gallant manner, the heavy accent that made each sentence so charming. His letters, his begging, his eyes.

All that—a joke. He had just been flirting. Those

beautiful words of love—a game. Perhaps he and the crew had placed bets on how much foolishness Flossie would believe.

He is at home, thought Flossie, among his brothers and cousins, laughing at me. I—like a stupid girl, like the whole history of stupid girls—believed every word he said.

Beautiful New York became grim New York. The magnificent horses pulling carriages were just huge sweating animals whose urine stank and steamed on the cobblestones. There was no soft romantic autumn air, just choking dust from cinder barrels that lined the sidewalks, waiting for pickup. Starched and courteous nannies pushing babies had gone home for tea, replaced by panhandlers and opium users.

She would stand on this terrible corner as the day turned to night, and warmth turned to cold, and ordinary street peddlers turned to threats in the dark.

A terrible desperation seized Flossie's chest, as if Johnny had stabbed her without drawing blood.

Could she go back and pretend this had never happened? Was it possible just to rejoin the wedding party? What explanation would she give? It was too late to pretend that a sick headache had prevented her from going down the aisle. And she had torn her gown. Her hair was ruined, her flowers abandoned. And by now the wedding was over. There was nothing to rejoin.

Oh, Johnny! I loved you! I was going to live with you. Your family would have been my family; your church would have been my church; your life, my life.

Her tears were hot and useless.

He had not come.

Flossie thought longingly of the grave. Only death seemed a possibility now.


"Get a grip on yourself, Dev," said Tod.

He was not treating her like a lady! He was treating her like—like—Devonny could not even say! Was this how men treated each other? This irritated refusal to help?

Since rescuing her from the seat belt, he had walked her through his terrifying house, demonstrating. How could anyone feel at home among so much machinery? It was like living in a factory. A tall glass box chewed food, handheld guns blew wind into the hair, a window box hummed while a dish circled inside, a large white box shuddered and groaned while throwing water over dishes, and most horrifying of all, a box of pictures talked by itself, while people who could not be seen laughed steadily.

"Here, siddown," said Tod. His speech was appalling. Slangy abbreviated orders. "We're gonna E-mail Annie, see if we can find out where Strat is. E-mail," he explained, "is kind of like your telegram, but you do it at home, and it has a different kind of address."

She was all right in the house as long as Tod did not leave her side, but he did not comprehend this and persisted in assuming that she would be fine on her own.

She could hardly wait till Tod's mother arrived. A woman to cling to.

"Don't say that!" warned Tod. "Women in our family don't cling. It's a rule of my mother's."

Devonny wanted to cry, but Tod made it clear that women in his family didn't cry, either. Well, she had seen Annie cry a time or two, but she would not betray Annie to her horrible mean cruel rotten brother.

"We're in luck," said Tod, "since my parents are at work. Mom doesn't go into New York on Saturday if she can help it, but today she had to, and Dad likes to straighten things up in his classroom when nobody's around, so he's gone too."

"For what article is your mother shopping?" asked Devonny.

"She's not shopping, she's at work. She's a stockbroker."

Devonny was delighted. "I wanted to be a woman of business!" she told Tod. "When I was little, I was permitted to go into Father's office and play secretary. Just before I was betrothed to Hugh-David, I asked Father for permission to start a telephone business, because I think those instruments will one day be used by all the wealthy, but he forbade me to discuss it."

"You're right about phones," said Tod, smiling, "and used by all the poor, too, and the rest of us in the middle. Maybe your father would let you be a lawyer, though, or a doctor."

Devonny laughed. "Who would trust a woman pretending to be a lawyer or a doctor?"

"Dev, we have a problem here. My mother will put a knife through you if you talk like that. And never use the word secretary in front of her. It's a swear word." He dropped heavily into a chair at a strange shiny desk.

Her father's office had typewriters, so she half recognized Tod's typing machine, but he did not use paper. The words came out in front of him on a blue window.

"Tell me what happened today, Dev," he said. The computer window flashed one picture after another. "How come you didn't want to marry the guy?"

"You'll laugh at me," she said, not wanting to tell.

So of course he did. His laugh was big and raucous, like a tied-up donkey. How vulgar he would sound to Lord Winden, and Gordon, and Miles.

She found herself liking Tod the way she had liked Annie: against her will. "When the man I marry walks into the room, I want my heart to feel as if John

Philip Sousa were directing a hundred marching bands, and all the drums were drumming and all the trumpets calling."

"No, huh?"

She shook her head. "Hugh-David is just a very well-dressed Englishman who needs pots of money to rebuild his estate."

"Was," said Tod. "He's bound to be dead by now. Whatever happened to him has happened."

Tod said this in his casual manner, as if it didn't matter. But it hit Devonny like a slap. Whatever happened to anybody she had ever known had already happened. They were all dead by now. A hundred years had passed. They had had their marriages, their joys, their failures . . . and now they had their graves.

The room swayed around her.

Oh, Strat! she thought. You must be here. You must save me. I cannot occupy a world without the people I love . . . or even the people I don't.

"So what about the dowry you told me about? The two million dollars?"

She shook her head. "There was no wedding. The contracts will be null and void. But had we wed, since I was the only living child, when Father died, the rest of the fortune would come to me, too, and my husband would control that. Lord Winden would have had all he could use. And more."

"You're not the only child if Strat comes back," said Tod. "What happens if we find Strat? Then he's the heir."

"I don't care about the money. There's enough to go around. I just don't want to be forced into marriage and sent overseas with somebody who can't bother to be nice to me." She lifted her chin a little. "Somebody like you."

Tod swung in his chair and made a face at her. "Hey, watch who you're calling mean! I rescued you right at the altar! You called, I came. Women! You can't please 'em."

He finished his typewriting. His machine was thin and flat and ran on electricity, as if Tod's fingers were too weak to depress the letters. She read over his shoulder.

Annie—
  Well, now I've been where you've been, and I would never have believed it, but your pal Devonny is here with me. I grabbed her right at the altar just before she said her wedding vows, and I guess the groom is still standing there.
  I don't know what to do with her, except bring her home and lie to mom and dad (following in your footsteps). She's looking for her brother Strat she says you took him home with you. Dev says only Strat can solve this. Answer ASAP.

115

This is a burden I don't need. I got places to go and things to do.

I am the burden he doesn't need, thought Devonny. The hateful men's clothing, the dreadful humiliating trousers, the terrible exposure of her body, Tod's awful machinery and harsh language, the only woman in the house a creature who would accuse Devonny of swearing if she used the word secretary—well, it was too much.

"Come on," said Tod. He bundled her out of the room, but there was no comfort in his touch. He could have been a policeman dealing with a striking worker. "We've killed most of a perfectly decent Saturday. I got a soccer game and I can't be late, their parents go berserk, as if I'm not reliable and trustworthy. Get in the car."

"The car?" she said fearfully. "But do we not await Annie's answer?"

"You'll get used to the car. I'll teach you to drive. You'll love it. Power. Everybody loves to drive. No, we don't wait for Annie's answer, because I don't know when she's gonna check her E-mail."

He smiled, a softer expression than his grin, and surprised her with a gentle hug, a brotherly hug; she was even more surprised to realize that she would have preferred a different sort of hug altogether.

All the ladies were weeping with fear for Miss Devonny Stratton's reputation and life, so Flossie's father did not object to his wife's tears. But he refused to let her tell about Flossie.

"We will not tell the police she is missing!" hissed Mr. Van Stead. "What are you thinking of? You told me you had her under control. As usual, you have done a very poor job of bringing up our daughters."

"I'm sorry," she wept. "Flossie has always been sneaky. But we must find her, because the boy is enclosed upon the ship. We cannot have Flossie alone in the city! Think of the dreadful consequences."

"Flossie will suffer whatever she must suffer. By morning she will be on the doorstep begging forgiveness. In the meantime, we will not have our names dragged into this scandal. Look at the reporters! Look at the laughing guests! Look at Hiram—he's taken his shoe off, he's beating the wall with it. He's going to attack the groom."

"But perhaps Devonny too had an unsuitable hope. Perhaps there is yet another stonecutter! Surely the girls are together. We cannot have poor Mr. Stratton crazed with fear when we might have the answer at hand. And Devonny's mother! And the unfortunate groom! We must tell!"

"We have three other daughters to consider. We

will solve this on our own. We will not have anything as vulgar as police in our private lives. I forbid you to speak."

This time Devonny did not flinch when the radio burst into raucous shrieking music. She did not cry out when vehicles swept past each other on the road as if going to war. She told herself she could do nothing until Annie had sent the reply explaining how to reach Strat. This was a temporary hell, and shortly her brother would save her. "Tell me," she said, "what is soccer?"

The topic made him happy. A soccer smile decorated his face, and for a moment Devonny rather liked Tod. She imagined him running around a field, in the midst of laughing little girls. It was so sweet. They would wear long flowered skirts, possibly even split skirts, with white stockings to cover their ankles.

"My team is sponsored by Laura's Fabric Shop, so be sure you root for Laura's. I'm only doing this because I have to, by the way. My mother is making me. The fathers only want to coach boys," said Tod, "so opening day of soccer season, the program was short of coaches."

The fathers will volunteer only for their sons, thought Devonny. So one thing has not changed in a hundred years.

The game included a parade of parents and critical observers. Laura's Fabric Shop was up against Sam's Garage, a group of six- and seven-year-olds from another neighborhood. It was immediately clear that Sam's included born athletes: girls who knew where the ball was. Tod's players might just as well have been wandering around Laura's Fabric Shop.

Tod stuck Devonny on the bleachers. Once he looked back at her, huddled and afraid, and he was furious with her, and furious with something else, too, though he wasn't sure what. He knew one thing: No girl on his team was ever going to cringe and shrink like that! He was going to have fighters! "Laura's!" he yelled. "C'mere. We're gonna win this one. I wanna see goals!"

But his little players clumped around the ball, preventing action. They're little, he reminded himself, I've got to be generous, and not yell at them because—

Letitia made a goal.

Tod had never expected such a thing. The girls recognized Tish's achievement and were wildly proud, hopping up and down and running to tell their parents.

Even Devonny was yelling, "Go, Laura's!" just like the parents.

He had to herd his team back on the field, because

they had assumed the game was over. They were surprised and a little irritated to find they had to play more. But they loved him, so they tried hard. Tod was surprised and a little irritated to find that he loved them back.

After the game, the little girls shrieked good-bye, and waved, and told their parents—for the hundredth time—"That's Tod, Mommy. Daddy, Daddy, look, there's Tod!"

"Oh, Tod!" cried Devonny as they got back in the car. She clapped her hands together prayer fashion, and stared at him worshipfully. "You were wonderful! The game was wonderful! I was allowed to run like that when I was little."

Normally Tod Lockwood was good at not thinking about things.

When his parents separated last year, he had carefully not thought about it. When his father moved in with Miss Bartten, Tod had thought about it briefly, removed himself, and stopped thinking about it. When he was clearly going to fail Spanish III, he had stopped thinking about it; and when he didn't have enough money for his car insurance, he had stopped thinking about driving, and instead thought about how to earn money. As each step of selling designer water collapsed, he stopped thinking about that, too, and moved right on to the next attempt.

The key to success was deciding what to think about. Discard the side issues.

Devonny Stratton had just stopped being a side issue.

When she beamed at him, proud of him, and when she bravely did the seat belt by herself, and when she said, "Pass that car, Tod," just like a regular person, who couldn't stand going a mere forty in a twenty-five mile zone, Tod had the most surprising daydream of his life.

Not money. Not power. Not school. Not sports. Not cars.

He wanted to kiss her.

He quickly turned his attention to the traffic. A guy let himself go down that path, he was finished. It was over. Tod was not falling into this trap.

Flossie had stood in one place too long.

She had attracted attention, something a lady without an escort must never do.

Two men sidled up to her. Dirty strangers with dirty fingernails and bad teeth. Depraved. A lady had male relatives to protect her from this.

Flossie did not move. Let them do as they wanted. She was ruined anyway.

"Miss?" said one of them. "You in trouble?"

She could not speak. No doubt this was the usual ploy, pretending to be kind.

"What's wrong, honey?" said the other man.

A street person dared address her in such familiar terms? Her father would have him whipped.

But if she went home, her father would have Flossie whipped. She could not bear it. She could not go home. She could not admit how stupid, how pathetic she had been. She thought of the rosy sunlit days at Devonny's, dancing behind a holly tree, kissing a letter, holding Johnny's cheeks in her hands. He shaved, but not closely, and when she touched him, it rasped her palms and made her shiver from limb to limb.

It had meant nothing.

"You look like you're gonna jump off the Brooklyn Bridge. You gonna have a baby and no husband? It's not the end of the world, honey. You go to the shelter for wayward girls, you have the baby and it goes into an orphanage and you have your life back."

A wayward girl, thought Flossie.

"Come on, we'll take you to a shelter. They got 'em for girls, you can't stay on the street."

She let the men walk her where they chose. In her fragile cloth slippers, it was a terrible journey. It hurt her feet, and hurt her heart. She did not know, and hardly cared, how they might hurt her body.

The pain of Johnny not showing up was so great that more pain hardly mattered. She deserved pain, acting without her parents' permission.

Whatever these men wish to do to me, she thought, I will submit. Girls must submit, and I have fought the rule.

"Extra, extra!" shouted the newsboys on the corners of New York.

They wore short pants, held up by suspenders. The sleeves of their white shirts were baggy and soft. Their bow ties were soiled and their caps were ancient.

But they sold a lot of newspapers.

BRIDE KIDNAPPED! said the headlines. GROOM OFFERS MILLION-DOLLAR DIAMOND NECKLACE FOR HER SAFE RETURN.

# SIX

𝒢ianni Annello had lost all his English.

Not a syllable would come to him. All his hard-earned language, his night classes, his immigrant studies. Gone.

He screamed in Italian. He kicked in Italian. He bludgeoned the door in Italian and then he broke everything in the tiny cabin in Italian.

It did not matter what language he swore in.

He was a prisoner.

On his wedding day, going to his bride. The money for their marriage certificate in his pocket. The slender gold ring for Flossie's finger, sewn by his mother to the inside of his vest . . . and he was a prisoner on a boat sailing to Europe.

He wanted to be like his father: a man who could be counted on. Flossie would be alone in New York as night moved in. A girl like that. And he, Gianni Annello, responsible!

Flossie was fragile. She had been cared for all her life and had never done a thing by herself. He thought of the rough edges of this city, and he thought of Flossie, who had never seen them, would not know how to handle them, could be raped or beaten, her clothes and jewels ripped from her slender body.

Once more he attacked the door, and once more the door remained solid against his thrashing.

He prayed: God, let Flossie not have the courage to leave the wedding after all. God, keep Flossie so afraid of her parents that she does not leave the church.

But religion was for women, and if there was a God, God knew that Gianni didn't believe.

Flossie would slip away and run to meet him in the square, for the romance and the danger of eloping had appealed to her fancy.

He hated himself. There truly had been danger, and he, Gianni, had laughed it off.

Flossie must rescue herself, but she was from a world where girls did not. He had not had time to teach her what his mother knew. It was his mother's courage that had picked up a suffering family, taken it to a foreign and terrifying shore, forced husband and sons to learn the English language and the American way. And in this hard hard country, in this hard hard world, Gianni's mother had not only reared her sons, but saved enough money to buy the four-story tenement in which they lived. There was nothing his mother could not face.

But Flossie . . .


Hugh-David Winden had read a wonderful book called *Beau Geste*, in which the hero (Beau was his nickname, because he was so handsome; did such a nickname suit Hugh-David also?) gallantly saved his aunt from disgrace by covering up her theft of a valuable gem. To cast suspicion on himself, Beau left England to join the French Foreign Legion and die a grim but brave death in the desert.

Hugh-David was not interested in the French Foreign Legion nor in death, but he wanted to be a hero. Surrounded by ruffians, he felt the need to demonstrate his noble heritage. He did not offer the diamonds for love, but because the gesture made him feel heroic. Or at least, facing in a heroic direction.

Having made the offer, and impressed the entire city, he suddenly wondered how he would face his family, having very possibly given Granny's pebbles to some cutthroat in Manhattan.

Miles and Gordon had drifted away. They could slither between scandals and remain untarnished. He was alone. Because a hero deserved comfort, he moved his belongings into the Waldorf-Astoria, a magnificent hotel he usually enjoyed.

He waited for the police to accomplish something intelligent, although they had not impressed him as capable of that. He found a deck of cards and began a favorite variety of solitaire.

It was not sufficiently absorbing. In his head rang the voice of his bride: I will marry a man with spunk. You are horse manure.

When they got home from soccer practice, Annie's answer was waiting.

Tod—

Wow! How are you going to handle the parents? Tell Devonny Strat did not come with me; I think he's an archaeologist in Egypt, although when I did library research about local history and the Stratton family, I couldn't prove it. Anyway, she's not going to find her brother in this century in our town. Did she actually jilt the guy at the altar? Way cool. Wish I had been there. Will he kill her if she goes home, and will she stay with us forever? I could use a sister. Don't let her leave til I get there.

Devonny clung to Tod, in spite of his yelling at her never to do that. *"Strat is not here? What shall I do, Tod? I cannot manage without him! He must be here!*

That's why I came! He must rescue me. And not just me! What about my mother?"

"You came to get away from the wedding," said Tod. "Nobody promised you Strat would be here. And you *have* to manage without him because he *isn't* here. Now stop whining. My mother just drove up, and she doesn't like people who aren't self-sufficient."

Nellie Fish loved her clothing: a simple brown dress, fitted at the waist, with plain long sleeves, and over the dress, a snow-white apron, so heavily starched it could stand up by itself. The apron reached the floor and tied in the back with a wide sash that stood out behind Nellie like a Christmas bow. Buttoned to the waist of the apron was a bib so heavily starched it did not bend, and its straps were wide and crunchy over her shoulders. Buttoned to the wrists of the brown dress were cuffs as rigid as the bib, and buttoned to the neckline was her gleaming white collar, solid with starch. Nellie's posture was vertical and rigid, to prevent any creases in the beautiful stiff starch of her beautiful stiff white uniform.

Her black hair was piled high on her head, stuck with a dozen pins to keep it there, topped by a tiny white ruff that marked her out for the hotel guests as their own personal floor maid.

She was stunned and thrilled to be maid for an English gentleman. A title! Think of it! Nellie had never been close to a celebrity before. It was wonderful. The gentleman's clothing was simply amazing. And when it turned out that this was the very Lord Winden whose bride had vanished from the church during the wedding march . . . why, Nellie was the most important person on the staff. Everyone was counting on her to bring back the details and quote the conversations.

Nellie was not going to let them down.

She was eighteen herself, and very pretty. What if her beauty overwhelmed Lord Winden? Perhaps in his hour of need and betrayal, she, Nellie Fish, would fill his heart.

But sadly, when she answered Lord Winden's ring, he was not alone: Another lady and gentleman had arrived. Nellie rolled in a cart for late supper and began arranging the linens and silver and crystal and flowers.

Not one word was spoken by any of the three guests. Nellie knew how to solve this: out of sight, a maid was out of mind.

Nellie bustled into the bathroom to check towels and be sure that the gentleman (because men were not gentlemen in the way they treated their discarded underwear) had not left an unmentionable on the floor, which would shock the lady should she be forced to enter this room.

Sure enough, the three began to talk, and Nellie

stood quietly, memorizing each word, as she folded and refolded the towels.

"Why, Tod, darling, I'm so proud of you!" cried his mother. "Of course you may stay with us for a few days, Devonny. How awful to have your host family turn out so rude and difficult. You may have our daughter's room. Her name is Annie. You can probably wear her clothes, too. She left a completely full closet here even though she shipped a hundred boxes."

Devonny had a wardrobe like that. She could ship a hundred boxes and still have a full closet. She smiled and tried to maintain her British accent and not inadvertently use a swear word like secretary.

"Whew. Dinner. Let's go to McDonald's," said the mother. "I'm whipped, I can't look a kitchen in the eye."

Tod whispered in Devonny's ear. "Restaurant," he explained.

Devonny had dined in public. Some of her best memories were the restaurants of Paris. "I shall put on a dress," she said happily.

"Darling," said Mrs. Lockwood, ignoring the dress idea, and swooping Devonny and Tod back into the dark and scary car stable.

They drove through fireworks. There were lights everywhere. Inside buildings, words were lit up in red

130

or blue. Huge signs stood by the side of the road, with their own lighting systems. Imagine having reading material stuck up in the air like that.

People's houses and offices were lighted, the streets were lighted, and most of all, the motorcars were lighted. Devonny had never imagined darkness without the dark. It was beautiful and wonderful. And a beautiful, wonderful thought came to her! Annie believed Strat was alive and well, digging up pharaohs in Egypt! So Annie had done her part—she'd saved Strat. But Strat was not here to do *his* part—saving Devonny.

The restaurant was appalling.

The tables were not set. There were no waiters. People kept their coats on and actually lined up to be given a tray of food, like beggars at the Salvation Army.

Devonny was horrified. Families were bringing children into a situation like this.

She did not recognize the food. She thought of Flossie—was she Mrs. Annello by now?—eating unknown foods with her new Italian family. She thought of Hugh-David, no doubt eating alone in his hotel room rather than facing the world that had seen him jilted; she thought of her mother—

My mother, thought Devonny Stratton. *My mother.*

She looked at Tod's mother, striding around, knowing what to do. Devonny's mother had never taken a step like that. Aurelia Stratton had never known what to do. The one step Aurelia took—threatening Hiram Stratton—had been the most stupid and dangerous of her life.

Devonny was not sure she loved a mother who could connive a hard fate for a daughter, and yet Devonny loved her mother completely. She forgave her without needing facts. This was her mother, and Devonny could not let Mama suffer.

I am caught here in this dreadful public place, thought Devonny, and where is my mother, and what can I do to save her from Father's wrath?

I can do nothing.

Tod grabbed a tray overflowing with packages but not food. He elbowed Devonny toward a tiny pretend table.

How much time had gone by on Devonny's wedding day? What was happening in New York at this very moment, a hundred years ago? Was Father punishing Mama? Was he using a physical method? He had been known to use his riding whip. He had used his belt on Strat often enough.

Mama could not endure such a thing. She was frail.

I am a prisoner as much as Mama, thought Devonny. She, nailed into the coffin of an attic, and I, shut into another century, where women must stand alone.

She fought tears while Tod unwrapped the packages. Sandwiches for dinner! How vulgar. Another package had little gold sticks, which Mrs. Lockwood salted heavily and began chewing on, one at a time. She used her fingers.

Devonny felt ill. A woman who considered secretary a swear word would eat dinner with her bare fingers?

Nobody had a fork. What had become of this country?

But she was terribly hungry. Desperately she gripped the huge round thing in both hands and chomped down like Tod. Onion and salad dressing and lettuce spurted onto her fingers. She stayed brave, continued to hold the sandwich and finished her bite.

"Why, that's wonderful," she said, astonished, staring down at the interior of the sandwich. "What are these called?" she said, forgetting she was English and should know these things.

"Darling," said Mrs. Lockwood, "you must live in a very rural area in England. Tell me all about it. Do you go to pubs and have shepherd's pie or do you stay home and have a joint of mutton?"

Devonny took another bite to give herself a little time to think. After all, everybody else was talking with a full mouth. Clearly, in this century people were barbarians. "We live in a castle," she said. "It's called Winden."

"Come on," said Mrs. Lockwood, laughing.

"She thinks you're kidding," interpreted Tod.

"No, no. The castle has two hundred rooms and is in desperate need of a new slate roof. We huddle in one corner, it's the only spot with heat and a bathroom." Devonny went on and on, quoting Hugh-David. The British accent began to feel familiar and pleasant. Mrs. Lockwood's fascination was delightful. Devonny felt like a social success. Even Tod was smiling. She finished her strange sandwich and wiped her lips. Papering her mouth, however, was not the worst moment of the dining experience. They had to clear their own table, as if they were scullery maids.

People paid money to eat here like this, thought Devonny.

She would not stoop to their level.

"Mrs. Lockwood," she said, inclining her head in a gracious bow, "I thank you for a lovely evening. I am most refreshed." She turned to Tod. She had a smile in her repertoire that men never failed to return. Indeed, Tod warmed under the sunlight of her smile, and returned it. "I am grateful for your rescue," she said, putting her hand lightly over his. "Your kindness overwhelms me. And how proud I was to witness your triumph on the soccer field."

---

Tod Lockwood fell in love.

He could feel it coming and tried to dodge. Love had such a sharp point that for a moment he believed in Cupid, complete with arrow. He actually ducked under the tiny table, pretending to retrieve a bunch of paper napkins, but he was trying to escape Devonny's smile.

No, he said to Love. Not for me. I don't have time. I'm not interested. Get out of here! Beat it!

He composed himself, straightened up and avoided looking at Devonny.

But it no longer took eyes to know that Devonny was there. He could feel her without touching her. Know her without focusing on her.

She was proud to witness my triumph, he thought.

A thousand other opportunities to triumph in front of Devonny Stratton invaded his imagination.

He felt his body heating up, his face changing color, his mind losing track.


Mrs. Van Stead had torn her handkerchief apart. The hem had come out quite easily, and then the lace, and now she shredded the linen thread by thread. Her lap was full of white debris.

Since it was her fault that Flossie had misbehaved, Mrs. Van Stead must whisper the ugly truth to Lord Winden. "Sir, another dread event occurred at the church. We think it best to confer."

Lord Winden shuffled his pack of cards in a noisy slapping manner. He could hardly control his irritation.

Mrs. Van Stead was accustomed to that in a man and she hurried on. "Our daughter Flossie fell in love with one of the Italian workmen putting in the stone walls and the fountain on the Stratton's estate in the country. We intercepted notes between our daughter and the boy. They had hopes of eloping."

The man actually smiled. "Ah, yes," he said casually, as if this did not matter, as if it were not the most awful thing to happen to a well-brought-up girl. "I remember how she would circle the bushes, as if we had not eyes to see, while the young man would ogle and flirt."

Mrs. Van Stead paled. "It was visible to all?"

"It was visible to me," said Lord Winden, shaking his head at the stupidity of young lovers. "What has that to do with my situation?"

Her husband acquired a voice. Mrs. Van Stead was greatly relieved. Men handled things so much better. "Naturally I had the boy rounded up and escorted to the hold of a ship I own," said Mr. Van Stead. "He will be taken back to Europe, although I would prefer to have him thrown off the ship while it is at sea."

"Clever of you," said Lord Winden.

"Today, before entering my pew," said Mrs. Van Stead, bowing her head over her lap of lint, "I personally checked my daughter's gown, hem, gloves and flowers. At fifteen minutes before the hour, my daughter stood with the other bridesmaids, awaiting the wedding processional. *But she did not come down the aisle.* Devonny is missing—and so is Flossie."

"I am so sorry," said Lord Winden.

"Had we but known Flossie planned to leave during the wedding and go to meet the boy, we would have restrained her," said Mr. Van Stead. "My wife is completely responsible for this laxity of supervision."

"Aha," said Lord Winden. He cut his deck of cards.

Mr. Van Stead saw that Lord Winden did not think very clearly, so he said, "I assume that Devonny has done the same, and also went to meet her Italian stonecutter."

The Englishman grasped the situation at last.

Nellie Fish stormed out of the bathroom, crisp apron flouncing. "Criminal!" she shouted at Mr. Van Stead. She shook her finger at him. "Evil man! Beast!"

They gaped at Nellie Fish.

"You kidnapped an innocent boy because your daughter wrote love letters to him?" shouted Nellie Fish. "I thought you were gentlemen! You are horrible terrible people. You do not deserve this dinner."

Nellie Fish flung the table on its side. Gravy splashed on the floor. A silver fork narrowly missed

Mrs. Van Stead. Crystal smashed against the brocaded wall. Pastry filling clung to a lampshade.

"*You* will stay here," commanded Nellie Fish. "*I* will summon the law."

She sailed from the room, as much starch in her spine as in her apron.

For a moment, it seemed reasonable to go after the silly woman and throw *her* into the hold of a ship, but even the Van Steads sensed that this was a bad plan.

Hugh-David was swamped with rage.

The woman with whom he had planned to share his life! his title! his castle! his bloodlines!—this woman ran away on their wedding day to some low-class, stone-dusted immigrant?

He had offered the diamonds as a reward, trusting that Devonny had been kidnapped, and all along she had meant what she said on the veranda: I would not marry you if you were the last man on earth.

He, Winden, would get this Italian and torture the truth out of him. "Show me this ship! We must force the boy to tell us where the girls expected to meet him. We will then pick the girls up. I shall return Miss Stratton to her father, who knows the true meaning of the word punishment."

"Don't hurt the boy," whimpered Mrs. Van Stead. She did not care about Gianni's fate, but what with hotel staff summoning police, perhaps murder or mutilation should not be added to their activities.

"All right, my dear. When I kill him, I shall do it swiftly so he feels no pain." Her husband glared at her. "Of course I'm going to hurt him! Defiling my daughter?"

Mr. Van Stead and Lord Winden stalked out of the hotel, even as Nellie struggled to find somebody, anybody at all, who believed her . . . even as Nellie was finding that yes, everybody believed her, gentlemen did that kind of thing, but nobody was going to take action. Did Nellie seriously believe the police would bother an English lord over some useless Italian going back where he belonged?

"Cab!" shouted Mr. Van Stead. A covered horse-drawn carriage pulled right up. The door was flung open for them, and the driver given his directions to the dockside.

Mrs. Van Stead sat awkwardly in a stranger's hotel room, staring at the china and silver upon the floor. She felt quite faint. Would it be proper to nibble on one of the pastries that had landed in a relatively clean position?

Flossie Van Stead recognized her surroundings. The men had walked her uptown, close to the train station. Why, whenever she visited the country, she took the train from Grand Central. She could take the train to Johnny's town in Connecticut only a few miles from the Strattons' seaside mansion.

Did she have the courage?

If Johnny had never had plans to wed Flossie, the Annellos would not even know her name. She would be a demented woman on their doorstep, making demented claims.

And what if Johnny himself was there, having dinner? Would she stand bedraggled and red-eyed on the stairs while he led the laughter?

But if she went to her own home, she would not be greeted by laughter. She could not begin to imagine what her father would do. She had never worried about this, because she had expected Johnny and all his kin to be at her side.

I have been such a fool, she thought dully.

And yet . . . and yet . . .

Surely it had been true love! Surely Johnny had meant to come! Surely when he talked of their lives together, the children they would have, the joy they would share . . .

But what excuse . . . ?

No, there could be no excuse. She just wanted him to have an excuse.

I must find out. I must face him. I must hear from his lips that this was a joke. How can I go to his family? thought Flossie. But how can I go to mine?

She had halted, and when at last she came to herself, she found her two escorts regarding her sadly. One of them patted her on the back, and the warmth and pressure of his touch brought her again to tears.

How could I have been afraid of them, she thought, when they are afraid for me?

She said to this rough pair, "Could you possibly lend me the fare for the train? I have friends to whom I can go."

The two men searched their pockets and wallets, uncertainly and with long exchanges between themselves.

They had no money. "I'm sorry," she said, sick at her lack of manners. "I shouldn't have asked."

They shrugged. Between them, counting carefully, they came up with train fare. They put the coins neatly in her palm, and her eyes overflowed. They had given her, quite literally, their last pennies.

For me, thought Flossie, a stranger, they will go without dinner, and perhaps their children, too, will go without dinner.

What beauty there was in the simple kindness of strangers. And she saw that in their ugly clothes, behind their dirty fingernails, they were heroes. Heroes whose names she did not know, and whose address she did not have.

"I promise to pay you back. Write down your addresses for me," she said.

They were oddly embarrassed. It dawned on her that they could not write. Might not have addresses.

They shook their heads and said not to worry about them. They asked God's blessing upon her journey. They took her to the right train and told the conductor to look out for her.

The train sped through the darkness, while Flossie Van Stead found light.

Whether or not Johnny loved her, she knew now that there was another direction in life. She, too, could be kind to strangers. She could do what those women starting settlement houses were doing—helping the poor. Flossie and her friends had laughed at such ladies: how ridiculous to spend perfectly good money helping immigrants.

But now she had been lost, penniless and deeply afraid.

I will not be a silly girl anymore, she thought. I will be a woman, and I will honor what these men have done.

On the way home from McDonald's, Tod's mother said, "Stop at the library, Tod." To Devonny she explained, "I read by the armload. The greatest disaster is to run out of library books. We'll just dash in, dash out."

"Not true," said Tod, "it takes her half an hour.

142

We'll go in, too, Dev. I need to do a little research myself."

Devonny had been asked to contribute to the new public library being erected in New York City, but had not. It was such a peculiar idea. A library intended for all New York City? There weren't enough people who knew how to read. Lower-class people didn't need books.

Yet one of her father's colleagues, Mr. Carnegie, was building libraries in every small town in America. The man was amazing in his dedication to books.

When the Lockwoods and Devonny entered the town library, Devonny expected to see a few shelves of darkly bound books by boring writers. She was stunned at the immense space. And on those shelves! Beautiful books! whole floors of books! books for babies and small children and people who gardened and people who traveled! There was a room for studying and a room for journals, and these rooms had the air of a men's club (although she had never been in one) with comfy big chairs sprawled around for silent thought and uninterrupted reading.

She was even more stunned to find a huge and wonderful music room with a bronze plaque over the door: GIANNI ANNELLO ROOM.

Flossie's Johnny? she thought. Her hair prickled. Her skin shivered with gooseflesh.

If I stay here, I will miss my life. I will not know if Flossie married this Gianni, if they had children, if those children honored their father with this plaque. I will not know. I will not see or laugh or dine with Flossie.

If I stay here, terrible things will happen to my mother. Father promised to destroy the letter writer, and I agreed that it should be done. He will relish the task. He will omit no pain or suffering.

Devonny wandered past a section called murder mysteries. Back home, there was nothing she enjoyed more than a good murder story.

It crossed her mind that nobody in her own time knew what had happened to her. Nobody could. Nobody would.

No trace of Devonny would turn up. No body. No ransom would be asked. No news of her marriage to another would arrive.

What if people thought it was murder? What if people said Devonny was on the bottom of the East River, cement weighting her ankles?

Who would be accused of this deed? Whatever weakling stood closest.

*Mama.*

Devonny stared around the unfamiliar building, with its incredible number of reading materials, and the astounding number of men, women and children using them. It was difficult to breathe or think. Mama—accused of murder!

She would be hanged.

Only my return can save Mama, thought Devonny. There is no Strat to save either of us. I must get home. I must cross Time again. It will be too late to pacify Father by marrying Lord Winden. Hugh-David will be long gone; he will be England-bound, correct in his assumptions about America: brutality and ruffians and violence and stupidity and bad manners.

I can save Mama from her fate, but I cannot save myself. I will have no explanation for what I did or where I have been. Father will shut me away just as he said he would.

It was a terrible choice.

For if she returned to her own Time, she would not return to the life she had led there, for she had destroyed it. But if she stayed here, and created a new life, in this Time, with these people, her mother would suffer a hideous end.

Gianni's mother spoke no English, and Flossie no Italian.

Mrs. Annello was short and fat, as gray as a great-grandmother. She pushed Flossie into a chair, taking off the ruined slippers, bathing her feet and preparing hot-water bottles. Flossie's decision to be a grown-up dissolved the moment she was treated as a child. She sobbed without stopping, while the Annellos kept saying, "Gianni? Gianni?" Flossie held up her hands in a universal shrug.

Mrs. Annello gave her something even more universal: a welcome. As if she were a daughter . . . a daughter who was expected.

At last a cousin arrived whose English was perfect. Flossie gripped Mrs. Annello's hands and told her saga to the cousin. "He just didn't come," she finished. "I waited and waited, and cried, and it was dark, and I could not go home, and I had to believe that Johnny meant to come. Then two strangers came over to me. They were badly shaven, their beards in need of trim, their collars filthy. I was so afraid of them, but they said they would take me to a shelter. And then I thought of just coming to you. I had no money for train fare. They pooled their coins, and put me on the right train, and made me promise that just because my lover did not appear, I would not jump off a bridge or hurt myself. They cared about me."

"We care about you," said the cousin stoutly, and Flossie wept even harder and said, "But where is Gianni?"

Where indeed?

———

Tod drifted away from his mother and Devonny to locate the reference librarian. "I need to know how much inflation has taken place since 1898, please," he said.

The librarian tracked it down speedily. "Multiply by thirty-three," she said, and moved off to help another patron.

Thirty-three times two million dollars was sixty-six million dollars. That was what Devonny Stratton would have brought to Lord Hugh-David Winden.

Wow, thought Tod. Bet he's pissed.

At the front desk of the great hotel, a telegram had been received and was awaiting the return of Lord Winden.

DO NOT OFFER HEIRLOOM NECKLACE TO AMERICAN PUBLIC STOP I WILL BE ON NEXT BOAT STOP DO NOT ASSOCIATE WITH STRATTON FAMILY STOP CANNOT FATHOM YOUR CHILDISH BEHAVIOR STOP
MOTHER

# SEVEN

*H*ugh-David did not travel far from the trusted
path, and that included the trusted roads of New
York or London. He would never have entered a
neighborhood in which he would not entertain.

The streetlamps which graced the nice side of town
did not exist near the docks. No one had shoveled the
horse manure from the roads. Rats and starving dogs
competed for garbage. A miasma of damp stinking air
settled over the carriage. Groups of men rustled half
seen and half sensed in black corners.

They could not find the ship.

Warehouses, huge and sprawling, ran on block after block. Immense stacks of enormous crates blocked
the way. Wharf after wharf lay empty, or its space
was filled with a garbage scow or a coal tub. Watch-
men yelled at them and beggars howled threats.

We are fools, thought Hugh-David. These people
live in shacks or in the street, with no money, no food

and no hope. These men I can only half see, they're wild unfed packs of dogs, and I with the chain of my pocket watch glittering gold in the night.

At last, at last, the ship that belonged to Mr. Van Stead! An ugly graceless heap. Its gangplank was drawn. They had to stand on the edge of the dock, while the filthy water slapped against the pilings, and shout through their cupped hands to get attention. Nobody believed the owner could be here.

They were inspected by the dim light of a kerosene lamp held grudgingly by louse-ridden deckhands.

Looking at the men he had hired, Hugh-David had to wonder if Mr. Van Stead was wise to admit being the owner.

Finally they were permitted on board.

In the yellow failing glow of that lantern, they walked on decks that tilted as if eager to endanger their balance.

It was far into the night before Hugh-David Winden and Elmer Van Stead finally saw Gianni Annello face-to-face.

Into the captain's cabin—mattress smelling of mildew, clothing bundled into corners without first being washed, a basin for shaving that had not been rinsed out in many months—a young man was brought.

Yes. It was the boy from the stonecutters' crew. And he had definitely intended to meet Flossie. He was not wearing the overalls, work shirt and boots of his daily life, but a dark suit, shiny with age, pitifully out of style, perhaps loaned him by a relative from another generation. It was torn now, stained from his imprisonment, but still a suit in which a man might get married.

Hugh-David waited while Mr. Van Stead screamed at Gianni. Mr. Van Stead had a long list of names to call Gianni Annello. He did not get far.

Nobody had expected Gianni to scream back. Gianni Annello leaped upon Elmer Van Stead, grabbing him by the neck. The celluloid collar came off in his hands. Gianni threw it aside and gripped the lapels instead, lifting Mr. Van Stead to his toes. Gianni's unshaven face was two inches from Mr. Van Stead's sculptured mustache. Muscles that lifted stone lifted a man without trouble.

It was not Gianni who risked being thrown overboard.

"You stopped me," said Gianni Annello, "without stopping her? You do not know where Flossie is? It is night, and she is out there alone?"

"It is your fault," blustered Mr. Van Stead. He had no hope of freeing himself.

"It is yours," said Gianni Annello, "and if anything has happened to my bride, I get you for it."

"I suppose you think you could call the law upon me," said Mr. Van Stead.

150

"I suppose that you will find a knife through your ribs, and it will be mine."

Hugh-David loved threats, and often made them himself. But he never followed through, and nobody ever thought he would. Gianni, however, was not making a threat. This was a statement.

Elmer Van Stead knew it, and when Gianni released his jacket, Flossie's father backed away, breathing hard and pretending not to.

"You just wanted Flossie's money," said Hugh-David, trying to gain control of the situation.

Gianni Annello stared at him. "No," said Gianni. "That was you marrying for money."

Hugh-David flushed. He could not believe he was being put in his place by some immigrant. He rallied. He had intended to torture the truth out of this weakling. Clearly, another approach was called for. "We came because my bride is also missing. Miss Devonny Stratton. She vanished when Flossie did, during the wedding march at the church. There is a claim that she was kidnapped, but when we found that you were involved, we thought you would know Miss Devonny's plans as well as Miss Flossie's."

In the dim light, Gianni looked shocked. "I know nothing," he said. The rough threatening voice was gone, replaced by anxiety. "I do not believe she had such plans," said Gianni, sounding young. "The only plan was for Flossie. They were so excited about it, the girls. It seemed to them full of romance and danger."

Lord Winden stared at the boy. "Then—she did not have— She was not interested— There was no young man—"

"No, sir. She spoke of the wedding vows she would take, and how they frightened her, but she was brave. Her father had made a threat to her, which she would not reveal."

It came to Hugh-David again that he was not the one who had insisted on having the wedding so speedily.

"What was this claim of kidnap?" said Gianni Annello.

"Mr. Stratton received a letter," said Hugh-David. He imagined the worst: savage curs who wanted a ransom and, until they received it, would hurt a beautiful young girl in every way there was to hurt. He imagined the best: that he had been jilted, and that Devonny was happy on her wedding night, but not with him.

There was space in his heart for horror: He would prefer Devonny caught in the terror of kidnap than safe in the arms of love.

I am not a gentleman, he thought.

"You have wasted time," said the boy to Flossie's father. "You have wasted this entire night. Even now you waste time. You are not looking for her." Gianni

152

opened the cabin door and strode out. "Where have you searched so far?" he demanded. They had no choice but to follow him. No choice but to admit that they had not really looked anywhere.

"Flossie is not first for you?" demanded Gianni. "You, her father?"

They had reached the deck, where the gangplank had been pulled back, and only the huge ropes attached the ship to the pier.

How restless was the night. Waves splashed, flags slapped, docks shifted, ropes creaked. Unless they were other noises—the gathering of gangs, the sharpening of knives, a bullet slid into the chamber of a pistol.

"Then—then where is Devonny now?" cried Hugh-David.

With the deckhands, Gianni maneuvered the gangplank back into position. "I would listen to the kidnapper, Mr. Winden."

"It is very dangerous here," said the captain. "The area is full of cutthroats. You must remain safely on board till morning. You are lucky you survived getting here."

Hugh-David shivered. On a cold and vicious night, some cold and vicious person possessed Devonny. And he, her intended husband? How cold and vicious was he?

Was she afraid? Hungry? In pain? Did she hate

153

him? Did she pray that he would come for her? Or did she know that Hugh-David was no hero, merely a man who pretended to give away diamonds?

"You must have quarters where we can sit in comfort, then, man," demanded Mr. Van Stead. "Take us there."

"Comfort?" said the captain. "On this ship?"

"Comfort!" said Gianni Annello. "You dare to think of your comfort? The father of a girl missing at night? My children will never know that you are their grandfather. I will not shame them with that." He went down the narrow wooden bridge and disappeared into the night.

On Monday, although Tod did not feel that Devonny was ready for high school, or that high school was ready for Devonny, he inspected her clothing, made her change out of a dress and into cords, shirt and pullover sweater, and put her in the huge old station wagon.

"Now we'll have to have another story for school," he said. "I don't know what we're going to do when the home story and the school story cross, but mostly my parents are too busy to check on things and mostly the school doesn't get around to it, either. So you're my cousin Devonny and you're here for a week, and you'll go to my classes. Don't say anything stupid."

"Saying stupid things is your role," said Devonny.

He grinned. Back home, Devonny thought, an insult had an effect: A cad tried to behave as a gentleman. Tod just enjoyed being insulted.

In school, however, she found that saying stupid things was universal. Who would dream that young gentlemen *and* young ladies would have foul mouths? Would shout rudely in front of their betters? And constantly talk back to their teachers!?

If Tod had disapproved of her clinging habit in his own house, it was clear that in school, should she cling to him, he would sever her hand from her wrist.

Students yelled and took quizzes and passed in papers and argued and gave excuses and turned on computers that spat out reams of information, and then the students leaped to their feet and charged down a hallway to do this again in another room.

In each room, an introduction of Devonny, a round of applause; a seat was found, a textbook shared. She had never encountered such complete friendliness. All of it was slightly rude. Many people said how sorry they were for Devonny, related by blood to Tod Lockwood.

But the clothing girls put on their bodies! The homeless of New York in 1898 did not wear the torn layers and hanging drooping shirts of the average girl in Tod's day.

Two girls asked if she wanted to go with them after

school to McDonald's. The students seemed to regard McDonald's as a club. She was touched, in a horrified way. But she did not want these girls for her friends. She wanted Flossie, and Gertrude, and Ethel. She wanted Harriett, who was dead, who had died so young from bad lungs.

But I am dead to my world, too, she thought, for they shall never see me again.

She was a ship without a rudder, doomed to drift on the sea of this harsh and demanding time.

Harriett had stepped forever through Time, and into Death. Could she, Devonny, step back? What threshold could she use to step back in Time?

She knew of none.

She let go, knowing herself a prisoner, and worked hard to do precisely what everybody else did, for it was her only hope: that she could fit into this Time instead of her own.

By the end of the day, Tod had been suspended from high school. Devonny was shocked to find that she, too, had been bad. "You didn't tell me it was wrong!" she yelled at him on the way home.

"Come on, Dev, how many squirt gun wars did you ever have in your living room?"

"Everything here is so ridiculous that I thought you probably did use the school auditorium for squirt gun wars."

"You had great aim, Dev. I loved how you went after the cheerleaders."

"They shouldn't paint their faces like that. I enjoyed soaking their hair." Tod laughed so hard he nearly drove the station wagon off the road.

Devonny grabbed the wheel and corrected his aim. "And staying home tomorrow is to be a punishment? In my day, if you disobeyed your elders, you would suffer a real punishment. You would be whipped, or confined to a cellar, or if you had my father for a father, you would be confined to an asylum." For the first time, something about Strat's torture was funny. "I must say that a person who sells squirt guns in school in order to market his designer water ought to be confined to a lunatic asylum."

Tod was indignant. "It was a great idea."

"You lost money on the water pistols."

"Well, nobody would pay me any more than I paid at the discount store. But I really did expect to make money on the water. I explained to everybody that the squirt guns worked only with Stratton Point Spring Water."

But his classmates had filled their pistols at the water fountains, and then had a squirt gun war in the auditorium on the day the state safety inspector was there.

This had not proved profitable in any way.

Tod stopped laughing after a while and made it home, and once they were inside the Lockwood house, Devonny was surprised by the silence. The family always had a television, radio, fax, phone, dishwasher, computer, or conversation going, or all at once, while they were doing whatever drudgery was necessary to keep their difficult lives moving along.

Tod fixed her a snack. He didn't work very hard at it. He opened a bag of potato chips, with which Devonny had fallen in love during school lunch, and they sat down together in front of what Tod said was a soap opera. Nobody sang and there was no soap.

Tod took her hand.

His hand was square and plain. It was scraped up from the last soccer practice, cut deep from sloppy technique in woodworking class, chapped red from his refusal to wear gloves.

She thought of Lord Winden, whose manicured fingers had held a horse's reins, or a fine fountain pen, but which would never scrape a dirty dish or change oil in a car.

"I'm glad you're here, Dev," said Tod. His hand had not entirely closed on hers, as if he needed permission for an actual squeeze.

Devonny Stratton did not hear a marching band. There were no cymbals. But if she faced in Tod's direction for a week, or a year, would she hear them?

Every instrument in joyful harmony? Would she fall in love with Tod Lockwood?

Had she crossed Time in order to meet Tod? Was he the reason? What great force, what incredible strength, could have ripped her from her own Time and brought her here?

She had taken too long. He panicked, and withdrew his hand, and hastily offered her a Coke, and jumped up to get it, and the moment was over, and she did not know how to get it back.


Hugh-David obtained the names and addresses of the stonecutters from Mr. Stratton's secretary. He sat at his hotel through several days of sleet and snow, but finally the weather cleared and he boarded a train to Connecticut. Here, in the fall, he had spent a delightful month at the Stratton summer estate, its towers glittering against the green sea and the blue sky. The Annellos lived only a few miles from the Mansion, and they too were on the waterfront. But theirs was a black and oily river, bubbling with sewage and dead fish.

He climbed to the third floor. A fat old woman opened the door and looked him up and down without approval. She called for others to come inspect and see whether this stranger should be allowed in.

"Lord Winden!" cried Flossie, darting forward.

"You're here!" he said, stunned.

"Of course I'm here. Where did you think I would be?"

Dead, he thought. Murdered, raped, thrown into a canal.

"When Gianni didn't come," said Flossie, "I knew something terrible had happened, so I came straight to his family." She beamed at him, as if they were friends; as if he had done good deeds in her presence. "*My* family now," she said proudly. She bowed her head and a flush of joy pinked her cheeks. She looked back up into Hugh-David's eyes. "We're married," she said, as if speaking the most beautiful words on earth.

Hands parted the babbling relatives. Gianni Annello moved forward. He stood behind his bride, wider, taller and stronger. Hugh-David was not sure how to behave. Slowly he extended his hand in congratulation, and slowly Gianni Annello took it. Flossie kissed them both, for now she was a married woman and need not behave so carefully.

"Now you must come in and have something to eat," she said, "and tell us everything you know about Devonny."

"I know nothing," he said.

Flossie cried out. "There has been no clue? No news?"

"Flossie, I continue to hope. I continue to hope

160

that perhaps she left as you did, for a finer embrace than mine. Because if that is not the case, then she is lost to us." He had not rehearsed that speech. It had come to him as he struggled to look Gianni Annello in the eye.

"You are being very brave," Flossie told him. "And I know that Devonny is being brave also. She did not seek any other arms than yours. She had promised her father. She would not break a promise."

They fed him.

Everybody ate, and ate a great deal, and the food was strange and delicious, cheeses and sausage he had not tasted before, and the rooms were hot with people and cooking and friendship. No matter how much they fed him, he felt a queer hunger, and by the end of the meal, he understood. He wanted this love and closeness, this worry and concern, these hugs and this noise: a family.

"I don't know," he said to Flossie, "if Devonny would expect anything from me. I don't know if she prays to hear my step, or if she wants to see me in the door of her rescue."

"She wants to see anybody at all rescuing her," said Gianni.

"Promise me you will continue to look for her," said Flossie. "She intended to repeat her vows: to love, honor, cherish and obey."

Cherish, thought Hugh-David Winden, and in that

moment he knew that nobody had ever cherished him.

"You, sir, must behave as if you, too, had taken those vows. Present or missing, Devonny Stratton is yours," said Flossie Van Stead Annello. "You must be faithful. You must save her."

Mrs. Lockwood was prepared to kill Tod for getting suspended, so Tod confused her by talking about how wonderful it would be for a British exchange student to have the splendid opportunity of going into New York City instead of school! Seeing a professional woman at work in a competitive and exciting field! Mom owed it to Devonny, to England, to Anglo-American relations, to take Devonny to work in the morning.

Mom fell for it. Tod thought maybe along with his career in designer water he would become a con artist, because if you could con your own mother in a crunch, you had skill.

Devonny was eager. She would see New York City a hundred years later! She would see if they really did have telephones. She would see what it was like to be a Self-Made Woman.

And she would see if on the right street at the right moment, she could mesh with Time and step back through.

Devonny had a parasol to match every dress. She

had petticoats of satin and lace and taffeta. She had white gloves to the elbow, a new pair once a week. She had miles of lace, ruffles and flouncing.

Devonny sorted through Annie's wardrobe to find something sufficiently dressy for town, but if there was any such thing, Annie had taken it with her to Norway. Annie's wardrobe consisted of dull dark colors in heavy hard materials, like the overalls of workmen.

Finally Devonny located a long flowered skirt and a blouse so large that nothing was revealed of her actual body, although it did not make her pretty, either. It was just cloth, and it was there.

"Perfect," enthused Mrs. Lockwood. "Now, I take the seven-oh-two train, so I will set the alarm for five-thirty."

In the morning? Yes, servants and cooks and tenders of heating systems got up at such an hour, but *people* didn't! "That will be fine," said Devonny, uttering one of her hugest lies.

And at five-thirty in the morning, they leaped from bed, showered, dressed, gulped coffee, rushed to the car, drove to the station, bought a ticket that cost as much as a week's rent, and finally sat crushed together on a rickety excuse for a train where nobody talked or had any fun but read a morning newspaper.

Devonny was thrilled to read the paper. Her stepmother Florinda was not permitted to read the paper, lest politics and threat of war upset her delicate balance.

They arrived at Grand Central Station (surely it had been much more grand?), took the subway, popped up out of the ground and walked several blocks to Mrs. Lockwood's office.

The buildings were so tall that Devonny could not think of it. What made them stand up? What if they fell? What if all that glass hit the pavement? How did you climb that many stairs?

But the streets were so clean—no horse droppings—and the cars so obedient to traffic fixtures. It was wonderful, how these people who did not know how to eat knew how to be kind in traffic.

The women had no sense of fashion. Black was the color of choice, or ivory or olive green. Was the nation in mourning? To Devonny's eye, they were dressing like men. She could not understand this. There were so few advantages to being a woman. Surely magnificent clothing was one, and these women had money of their own, which was most rare, but they were not spending it on clothing. Or if they were, they were making poor choices.

Not a single individual wore white gloves. Devonny could not imagine occupying an urban world and touching it. Why, you would have to wash your hands constantly!

Mr. Stratton requested the honor of Lord Winden's presence at his town house for a discussion of the choices now available to them.

Sitting frozen and terrified in the parlor was the first Mrs. Stratton.

Hugh-David bowed. "Madam," he said, "how you must be suffering with anxiety, even as I am."

"Her suffering," said Hiram Stratton, "is nothing compared to what it will be."

Hugh-David raised his eyebrows.

"Aurelia, tell the man what you have done."

Hugh-David moved closer to her, for if he could not be the hero that Flossie expected, at least he could be encouraging to Devonny's mother.

Mrs. Stratton was trying not to sob. "First, sir," she said to Hugh-David, "I shall tell you what Mr. Stratton has done. Perhaps you heard mention of our very dear son, Strat."

"Aurelia!" said Mr. Stratton dangerously.

"I shall tell him all of it or none of it," said Aurelia.

Mr. Stratton shrugged.

Hugh-David felt chilled. Surely this man never shrugged about anything, ever, in this world.

"My husband was very angry with Strat a few years ago because Strat had fallen in love and was full of silly stories about  girl named Annie. She was some sort of tramp and disappeared one day. Strat was deeply upset and said all manner of ridiculous things and argued strenuously with his father and with various household guests. He behaved badly. Arguments escalated. Soon anger between them had reached a fever pitch, and my husband felt he was no longer in control of his child. He took his revenge by pretending Strat was insane."

Hiram Stratton looked amused. He locked his fingers together on his large distended waist and rocked on his heels, contemplating the ceiling.

"He had our son locked up in an asylum to teach him a lesson. The lesson was: Never argue with your parent. Obey. Do not talk back. But Strat managed to escape, and there was a terrible accident, and my darling boy, my sweet and lovely son, was killed."

Hugh-David found himself kneeling, holding her cold hand between his. A father so harsh that he pretended the family blood was ruined in order to make a point? No wonder the poor woman's face was lined with sorrow.

Would Devonny ever have told Hugh-David where and how Strat had died? Would they have reached such a point of trust?

A line of sorrow formed on his own, much younger, face. For he had made it clear to his bride that she was not to waste time trusting him; she was simply a conduit for the money he needed.

"Have no respect for me, sir," said Mrs. Stratton

quietly. "Divorced and unnecessary in life, I was desperately lonely. I was not permitted to visit my children. My allowance was so small I could scarcely afford to leave the house, let alone attend the symphony or the opera. I could not afford the fashions necessary to pay visits or reply to invitations. Eventually, there were no friends and no invitations. My life was dark and cold."

He, too, hated dark cold corners, and stayed at his club, or traveled, or invited houseguests in order to warm himself by their conversation.

"So I arrived at a decision," said the mother of Devonny and Strat. "I would blackmail Hiram. In that letter, I would write that if his son had tainted blood, so did his daughter. Were this dread fact to be made public, no man would marry that daughter, lest the children of the marriage also be insane. Hiram believed the threat," she said, sounding proud of herself for writing such an effective letter. "He seized upon you, Lord Winden. He flung that wedding together in days. His scheme was to put you two on a ship and get you out of the country before this hideous truth became known. While you were getting Devonny with child, he would track down and destroy the blackmailer."

Hugh-David had thought himself sophisticated; he had thought little would shock him. He was shocked.

169

His own mother, who would manipulate anybody anywhere for any end, might have stopped before doing what Aurelia Stratton had done.

She rushed on with her wicked tale. "I was sure he would never find me out. I was sure that Devonny, given control of her fortune, would bring me to England, and I would be part of the new family! And I would have parties and fashions and friends and joy and music once more!"

Hiram sent the wrong one to the insane asylum, thought Hugh-David. She is insane from poverty. Insane from the loss of her son. "It worked well, Mrs. Stratton. But where is Devonny now? Did you arrange this also?"

The little woman gave him a strange clear look, past grief and fear, as if she had abandoned both her hope and her body.

His anxiety grew huge. It seemed to fill the room, like some noxious air. What had the woman done? What had they all done—he and the father and the mother—in their greed and selfishness?

"I know nothing of what has happened to Devonny," she said. "This has ruined me. My carefully laid plans—someone has destroyed them."

She did not care what had happened to Devonny. She was concerned with her ruined plans.

Oh, Devonny! he thought. No one knows where

you are. No friend, and no foe. I too have been an instrument in your suffering. Nor have I accomplished a thing. What park or room or alley am I to search? How to storm the city? Where is the mysterious letter, from which I could divine what cellar or garrett holds you prisoner?

But the days had passed. A kidnapper who did not care about a diamond necklace was not going to write in for a ransom. Hugh-David thought of Aurelia's dark insanity, Hiram's cruel fatherhood, Strat's lonely death, Devonny's unknown fate.

My mother will soon arrive, he thought, and will terrify everybody in sight. Including me.

He remembered telling Devonny she would be fine in England as long as she submitted to everything her mother-in-law said. But nobody was really fine around Hugh-David's mother; in fact, most people related to this woman spent their lives trying to avoid her.

I was going to use my wife to stand between me and my mother, he thought. Use Devonny to soak up my mother's temper and demands and thoughtlessness.

The tally of the ways in which he had planned to abandon Devonny was mounting. His opinion of himself slipped downward in proportion.

He left the splendid building that housed the failed

Stratton family, wishing that something as simple as joining the French Foreign Legion would save Devonny. But that was in books. In life, in the city, on the street, he did not know how to find her.

Nobody came to claim the necklace.

Except his mother.

# EIGHT

$\mathcal{M}$rs. Lockwood came to soccer practice the following Saturday.

It wasn't half so much fun with her there. How could Tod be a big important strong coach when his own mother was pacing around and making suggestions, which in her case were mainly orders? He was just a teenager doing an assigned chore.

"Do we have enough money to buy everybody an ice cream, Mrs. Lockwood?" asked Devonny. "Let's go to the store and get ice cream treats for the whole team."

Mrs. Lockwood thought that was an okay idea. Tod thought it was brilliant, and he smiled at Devonny, a smile that made her think twice about the twentieth century.

Devonny managed several detours to lengthen the errand. She needed to see how the high school game was coming along; she must dart into the pharmacy for lip balm and stop at home to get warmer gloves.

When they got back to the field, Tod and the Laura's Fabric Shop team were huddled around the bench, creating a strategy nobody could do and nobody would remember.

What a father he will be to his daughters, thought Devonny. What a husband he will be to his wife.

She was overwhelmed with wanting to be a good wife and a good mother, and to do these things with a good man.

At home, thought Devonny, men "do." Girls "are." But I'm watching a dozen little girls who not only expect to "do," but are being trained to "do" and love it. They will be like Tod's mother; they will run their team and make their goals.

What do I want?

Do I want to stay here and "do"?

Or do I want to go home and "be"?

She laughed painfully. She had no choice; Time had made it for her. These little girls on Tod's team: for them, the whole world was a choice. It was frightening to Devonny how much possibility lay ahead of these girls.

Yet they led such hard lives, these people!

They did not commence the day by drawing a serene hot bath, but leaped into a vertical box with a waterfall of water, cleansing in seconds. Then they leaped out and dressed themselves, and was there a hot meal awaiting to break the long fast of night? No. In the kitchen (kitchen! a lady had no place in a kitchen) you made your own (cold) breakfast.

And in class! The amount you were supposed to know!

It was undignified. There was no leisure. There was no elegance.

In Tod's school, the girls were tough. They whipped each other in sports, they aced exams, they chaired committees, they won science scholarships, they got into superior colleges, they even got into West Point!

They did not cling. They did not demurely await a man's pleasure. They were not demure.

After school, either they worked at a fast-food place or went there and had the fast food served by friends. Devonny would truly rather be dead than bring other people food or clean up after them.

Then the whole family had to work together to come up with dinner. Devonny herself was made to peel a potato.

Now they wolfed this food down and then sat in front of a television to watch other people talk and sing and dance while they did homework, and then they went to bed with no assistance. No one had

175

freshened the room, nor fluffed the pillows, nor prepared a hot-water bottle, nor filled the bedside carafe with cold water.

The day is going to come when Mrs. Lockwood will insist she has to call my supposed parents in England and tell them how much she loves me and what a fine guest I am, thought Devonny, and what will we do then, when we have to admit there is no family?

Family.

The cold burn of anxiety hit her again.

Oh, Mama, what are you suffering? You have made your terrible bed and must lie in it, and I took one great terrible step across Time and must accept it also.

"What's the matter, sweetie?" said Mrs. Lockwood, all concern, all hug.

Devonny found herself close to tears. "I feel very alone."

"It's difficult to cross an ocean to another country, I'm sure," agreed Mrs. Lockwood.

If she knew how great the ocean was! "You are so good at doing things by yourself," said Devonny. "Everybody here is so good at striding forward alone."

"Alone?" said Mrs. Lockwood. "I'm not alone. Alone is hard and awful. Nobody wants to be alone. I have made a great sacrifice and many compromises so that I will not be alone, Devonny."

Devonny did not believe this. "Tod says I'm a weak-minded Victorian who can't stand on her own feet."

"Where does he get this Victorian stuff, anyway? He keeps throwing that word around."

"I cannot imagine," said Devonny, and she kept her composure by distributing ice cream, while she imagined Victorian stuff: her world, her life, her friends, her family; the fiber of her soul.

There were three towers in the immense brown-shingled summer mansion by the shore. One was splendid, with a telescope and writing table for jotting observations of weather and natural history. It was not frequently used; not since a guest had been shot here last year.

One tower was part of the master bedroom, and Hiram's fourth wife frequently fled to the sanctuary of that high place. Hiram could not follow, because his bulk was too great for the tiny winding stair.

But the third tower was simply to match and look graceful. It was inconvenient and not used for anything. It was reached by stooping through a low attic.

The carpenters had nailed wood over the windows.

A cot was placed against one cold wall, where the chilly winter wind sifted through the cracks. A chamber pot, a Bible and two blankets had been placed by the cot.

The door had been flimsy, but now was strong, and bolted from the outside.

"You will be fed," said Hiram, "you who threatened me. But you will not have a life."

He slammed the door hard, slid the bolt so that it shrieked, smacked a servant who did not get out of his way and smiled to himself. Aurelia was out of his life—and out of her own—as if she had never been.

Downstairs, servants were covering the furniture with white sheets. Silver was packed to be taken back to New York for the winter, while crystal and china were shelved in the butler's pantry to await the spring. Rugs were rolled up and carried outdoors to be hung on lines and beaten clean. Horses were taken from the stable to board in town until Hiram needed them again next year.

Hiram strode out of doors to consider his view instead of his problems. As usual, the view entertained him not at all, and he was back to his problems.

It had felt good to see those hammers swing and force those nails forever into the window frames; it had felt good to see the fear and resignation of that old shriveled woman who had tried to damage him; but it did not feel good to stand here and know it accomplished nothing.

Nobody had accomplished anything.

His silly wife, Florinda, occupied herself writing letters to everybody they had ever known, especially in California, hoping for a clue to Devonny's whereabouts.

Police interviewed, scoured, searched, came up empty.

Lord Winden, skittering around with his necklace and his horrifying monster of a mother, was not capable of finding anything.

Flossie, in her new slum with her ridiculous husband, bringing shame upon her family, claimed to have no knowledge.

The police were skeptical that there was a kidnapper. After all, they claimed, Mr. Stratton should be able to supply more detail if such a person had actually penetrated the church and seized his daughter right off his own arm.

The wind rose. A flag snapped as hard as a snare drum.

There was no heat in the tower. It would be a long winter for Aurelia. Possibly she would not survive.

What have my children done to me? thought Hiram Stratton, his golf course and his gardens and his new fountain giving him no pleasure. A worthless son. A worthless daughter. I shall end up like my colleagues, having to give my fortune to some foolish university or worthless museum!

He had lost his son and now . . .

The truth came to Hiram Stratton.

He began laughing.

His laughter rose with the wind, and he knew it would be heard in the tower, for its walls were thin.

The kidnapper, somehow, some way, had been Strat himself! The son who stormed off, pretending death, refusing his heritage, had taken his revenge by taking his sister. Strat had ripped his sister right out of the church.

Hiram was suddenly quite proud of the son he had discarded. The boy has guts, he thought.

He stopped worrying about Devonny. Soon she and her brother would be in touch with him, and they would want money, and he would bargain until he had what he wanted: their marriages and their offspring.

Once more his step was jaunty, and he left for the city, and gave no more thought to the tower and the coming of winter.

Aurelia Stratton accepted her fate. She deserved it. She had done a horrible thing to her daughter. She had had no conscience, just a selfish desire for her own comfort.

This was how a worthless relative was treated. The severely brain-damaged, the grotesquely deformed, the emotionally crippled, the evildoer who belonged in jail but whose jail sentence would bring shame upon the household. Society agreed that such people belonged in the cellar or attic: lock them up, tell nobody they still existed, everybody would pretend they never had, and nobody would be forced to think of them again.

And now one of those people was Aurelia herself.

She heard the roar of laughter from the man who had fathered their two children.

She heard the carriage leave, heard the creak of wheels and the clatter of horses' hooves.

And then there was silence.

Only a few servants occupied the Mansion in winter. She had not seen them when the door was shut upon her.

They would bring her cold food only: there would be no sugar on the oatmeal, no salt on the meat, no drink except water, no butter for the bread, no hot coffee, no comforting soup. She would see no person. Whatever was handed in she would take, and whatever she handed back, empty bowl or full chamber pot, would be carried away. But she would see no sky, hear no person speak, have nothing to think about but her own failures.

She had slipped a note to the coachman. She could not include a bribe. She wondered if the note would be given to Hiram. Or had it already been given to him, and that was why he howled with laughter?

---

"We most certainly will not!" shouted Hugh-David's mother.

Hugh-David winced. Really, he had been upset with the rude bellowing of Americans, but his mother could bellow as loudly as any New Yorker.

"I believe I must," he said, trying to hold his ground.

"The woman is immoral. Evil. Disgusting. I am deeply disappointed in your silliness! Throw that note away immediately and stop whimpering over it."

Hugh-David did not think he had been whimpering. He had been considering. Considering a girl who once said that he had no spunk.

"Just what do you think you will do with the woman once you rescue her?" shouted his mother.

"I don't know," he admitted.

"Well, come up with something before you embark upon a ludicrous and unlawful excursion!"

Hugh-David yearned to nail his mother in a frigid attic. What pleasure there would be as he walked away. He reminded himself that he was not a barbarian, and must honor his mother.

This was a dreadful thought. The woman was bound to live for decades.

He said, "I am concerned that Aurelia Stratton might take her own life."

"What difference would that make?" demanded his

mother. "Her life is as good as gone anyway. It will save everyone a deal of trouble."

He took a deep breath. With his mother around, his lungs got as much exercise as if he had taken up rowing. "I do not think she did enough to deserve such a fate, Mother," he said, "and I do not think Devonny would wish to see her suffer. Certainly Devonny would not wish to see her die by her own hand. Devonny has a good heart. She would wish her mother's happiness and prosperity."

"A good heart?" shouted the Duchess. "A wench who runs away from her own wedding?"

"I cannot find or save my bride, but at least I can save her mother," said Hugh-David. "A gentleman does not abandon a lady." This was his new credo, difficult to remember when his mother was there. Some people deserved abandonment.

"Pshaw!" shouted the Duchess. "She abandoned you!"

His mother meant Devonny. "I don't think so, Mama. I think Hiram Stratton set this up. I understand nothing, but I will wait this out."

"What might you mean by that stupid remark? Do you plan to wait a month? A year? A decade? Come to your senses. You're like your father. Your blood is thin."

He studied his mother as she ranted and raved

about Granny's pebbles, which he had put at risk, and his duty, which he was failing, and America, which was annoying, and what should she wear to the party tonight in order to look better than anybody else.

Devonny's blood could be no worse than his own.

He opened the sad little scrawl from Devonny's mother and read it again.

"Let's drive down to Stratton Point, Tod," said Devonny. Gianni Annello has a music room named for him, and we have a town beach and park named for us, she thought. Did we become friends? Of course we didn't. I'm not there.

She had been deeply anxious all day, and now anxiety ruled her body. She could not eat, she could not look at the television, she could not go for a run with Tod's mother (a woman past her prime, a woman over forty, running up and down like a street boy!).

Devonny thought of her own mother, and a horrible sensation attacked her body. She felt the attic. The splinters on the wall pierced her hand. She trembled in the total dark. The lonely silence gnawed the edges of her sanity.

Tod was always willing to go for a drive, and he did have to obtain more designer water from the pump, so off to Stratton Point they went.

Devonny clung to the seat belt that had once frightened her so. How eerie to drive on paved roads where there had been a dirt path, to pass parking lots where there had been meadow, and—most awful—gaze up at a hill on which there was nothing but grass. A hundred years ago, she had danced in a ballroom there.

Her life was cut to the ground, not a trace remaining except the old red pump where the spring never ran dry.

"I'm going to teach you how to drive while we're here," said Tod. "There's nobody around except joggers and runners, and nobody needs them anyway; we'll just mow 'em down. You get extra points."

Devonny was used to this talk now. In Tod's Time, nobody meant anything by their threats, whereas in her Time, when Father threatened a person with being chained up . . . it happened.

She said, "I like having a chauffeur. You drive and I'll look out the window."

So he drove, and she looked out the window.

At the top of that graceful hill, a hundred years ago or perhaps now, her mother was afraid, alone and cold.

Tod had the excellent heater of the big old station wagon blasting; he himself was wearing a short-sleeved T-shirt. Yet Devonny felt the cruel wind slip beneath the shingles, cut through the blankets and lay frost upon her skin.

"Tonight Mom is taking us shopping," said Tod. "She says you have to have jeans that fit."

They are refitting me so that I am part of their Time. I should thank Tod, and love him forever, but I want to go home.

"Pretty soon we're going to have to explain why you don't have any family sending you spending money. I haven't thought of an explanation. Have you?"

Devonny was not thinking.

She was seeing.

There was a tower.

There were three towers.

There was a mansion.

Her long thick hair lay heavily on her shoulders. Her eyes burned with staring. She was afraid to point it out to Tod. Perhaps he had not noticed.

Had they driven through Time this Time, instead of falling?

Was Time now a simple matter of taking a road?

She was trying to listen, trying to hear her own century.

From somewhere, for some reason, some Time was calling.

The tower was supported by two crossing beams above Aurelia's head. She dragged the cot to the mid-

186

dle of the room and stood on it, measuring the distance.

Then she sat back down on the cot and methodically ripped the sheets in strips, weaving them for strength.

She was afraid she did not have sufficient courage. But she knew she did not have enough courage to face this life of confinement.

"O my son!" she cried out loud. "O my daughter! What courage did each of you need? And I was not there when you needed me. I contributed to your sorrow."

She clung to the torn edge of the sheet and said to her Maker, "I have sinned. Please forgive me. Please let me come to You in spite of my sins and in spite of what I am about to do."

"Stop the car," whispered Devonny. "I have to get out."

Tod said, "Dev, it's freezing out. You didn't wear a coat."

She got out of the station wagon.

Tod leaned on the horn.

"Stop it!" she shouted at him. "Stop making any noise!"

He stared at her and got out of the car, too, closing his door carefully so there was no slam. She was look-

ing everywhere. She was touching air, she was stepping around things that did not exist. "Dev?" he said
nervously.

"Let go of me," she said to him.

"I'm not holding you." She's there, he thought. In
her Time. She can see what I can't, touch what I
can't, hear what I can't.

He was deeply afraid, and he hated his own fear.
"Dev," he said, wanting to hold her safe from pain
and fear, wanting her to stay, and be his.

She was strangely blurry.

"No," he said, "you've come such a long way, Dev,
and you came for a reason, and we haven't found it
yet! Dev, don't go."

"Let go, Tod," she pleaded, although they were
yards apart. "I need to go home. I was wrong and you
were right. A lady cannot wait for a man to rescue
her. A lady cannot be weak-minded. She cannot demand that somebody else do something! A lady must
rescue herself."

Tod's lips were numb and his hands stiff.
"Devonny," he said, and he thought, I wanted to rescue her.

Devonny turned to him and she was clear again;
she was herself and beautiful and gold and—he was
surprised by this—strong.

"Whatever is wrong when I get there, Tod, whatever I suffer, whoever hurts me, whatever my father does—none of that matters."

He was the one who hurt. He hurt all over, as if she were beating him up.

"You told me I must stand alone," she said.

I didn't mean it, thought Tod, trying to approach her again, trying to take her hand. He thought of his mother, when divorce seemed imminent, shrieking at Dad that she was just fine alone! fine! go! see if I care!

But she cared. And she had not been fine alone.

Alone was hard.

He did not want Devonny to go alone into whatever Time was, and he did not want to be alone here.

He wondered where Strat was. Alone? And where would Devonny be? Alone?

*And where am I?*

"Let go of me, Tod," she whispered. "You are keeping me prisoner."

"No," he said, shocked, "I never did that, I never meant that. I was only trying to help."

So he let go. He had touched her only once, and yet he had to unwrap his daydreams and release his half hopes, and let go.

There was a gust of wind, as fierce as a hurricane, and he closed his eyes against it, and hunched his shoulders, hearing screams that were not his, pressed against shudders which were the suffering of others, and when it ended and he could open his eyes, he was alone with the grass and the wind and the seagulls.

There was no Devonny.

For a long time Tod clung to the edge of the car, waiting. It grew dark. There was nothing left to wait for.

He drove home.

# NINE

*L*ord Winden had meant this to be clandestine. He had intended to hire a carriage, travel at dusk, browbeat the few remaining servants, and then, soft and strong in the dark, carry the first Mrs. Stratton to safety.

He had most certainly not intended that his mother would notify Hiram Stratton, and Mr. Stratton would come with his fourth wife, Florinda, a silly little creature whose assets were unknown, and that Mr. Stratton would bring not one but two attorneys, and his own mother, the Duchess, would come along with her maidservant and with Gordon and Miles, whom she had adopted as her escorts in New York.

"I forbid you to do this!" shouted Mr. Stratton. "You may not enter my home!"

Hugh-David entered. The police had been so breathtakingly courteous during the church episode that he was confident they would not dream of arresting a man with a title. His title was minor, almost meaningless, and nobody in England cared, since everybody (especially his own brothers) came ahead of him, but here they did not know that.

He had always wanted some great expedition, some new world to conquer. He had thought possibly of exploring the Amazon or reaching the South Pole. Possibly joining one of the splashier commands in order to defeat mountain tribes who did not want to become Queen Victoria's subjects.

Breaking down an attic door was not world-shaking. Gordon and Miles were smirking, preparing yet another story to tell London about pathetic old Hugh-David. Perhaps Devonny was correct and he was horse manure.

There was an incredible amount of commotion. Mr. Stratton was yelling. The attorneys were yelling. The Duchess was yelling. Servants were yelling. The fourth wife was yelling.

"I do not know why you are making all this racket," said Hugh-David with as much dignity as he could muster. "I am simply going to see that my fiancée's mother has proper housing. Please lower your voices and behave in a reasonable manner."

Nobody took this suggestion.

They entered the huge Mansion. What had been beautiful and romantic by summer was grim and haunted by winter. The floors creaked and groaned.

The servants carried lanterns, which cast shadows, creating hollows and pits where none existed. The flat floor felt treacherous, as if it might tilt beneath his feet like the deck of the ship where Gianni Annello had been imprisoned.

"If you think I am going to take on the burden of some divorced creature, you may think again!" shrieked his mother.

His manservant had armed him with a hammer but Hugh-David had no idea how to use the weapon. Luckily, the same servant had whispered in his ear that all he really needed to do was slide the bolt on the attic door. Hugh-David reminded himself that it was not his mother on whom he would use the hammer.

"Stop this!" demanded his mother, planting her ample body in front of him. "We are returning to England before you make an even greater fool of yourself."

"I will return to England when Devonny is found."

"Why are you doing this when I have expressly forbidden it?" demanded his mother.

He found the great stair. He could see none of its colors in this dark, none of its riches and splendors. It was colder indoors than out. How could that be? Hiram Stratton's cruelty to his ex-wife seemed especially horrible because it was so cold.

"I'm doing this," said Lord Winden, "because it is right."

Gordon burst out laughing. "If you could see yourself, Hugh," he said. "You look utterly ridiculous, storming across America to rescue some shriveled-up old prune as if she were a beautiful golden-haired princess."

They were at the bottom of the great stair. The cold swirled down from the height of the open shaft, so fierce and dreadful they looked up, half expecting icicles on the chandeliers.

There stood the princess.

Screams rose in their throats, choked back from fear of what they were screaming at.

It was a specter. A dark ghost. A thing of medieval horror and power.

It was Devonny.

Hugh only half recognized her, for she was garbed in some sort of trouser, like a barbarian in the hills. Her lovely hair was loose, and somehow dusty, and disarranged. She stood silently above them and he felt a tremor, as if they were her subjects, and had disobeyed.

"Where did you come from?" he whispered. "Are you all right? Have you been here all along? *Did your own father lock you in the tower with your mother?* What is going on, Devonny? Please forgive me! I did not think of looking in your own house."

Behind Devonny stood her mother, a wraith more real.

Down they came. Step by step. Slow as a wedding march.

Hiram Stratton backed away. He mumbled, "No, that's not true, I didn't do that, it isn't me, it didn't happen." He tripped and fell heavily.

Devonny asked Hugh-David, "You were on your way to save my mother?"

"Yes," he said. He was numbed by her loveliness, shocked by the garb her father had forced her to wear. The audacity of the man! First imprisoning the son, then the former wife, finally the daughter! To what end? For what reason?

For a long while she did not speak. She paused three steps above him and examined the face of the man she had been destined to marry. He stared back. He was stronger than he had been. Standing up to his mother was an act he had never expected to achieve, and he had done it, and let Gordon and Miles laugh. He was stronger. Devonny, too, was stronger. Not weakened by her ordeal, she was calm and certain, standing in judgment of him.

"We have all suffered enough," said Devonny. "Let us not accuse one another of crimes and cruelty."

Hiram lurched to his feet. "But—"

"Let us forget the past."

195

She is a great lady, thought Hugh-David. Her wedding destroyed, her place in Society battered, her reputation suffering, her father responsible for her terrible fate—and she wants us to forget this. "I am impressed, Devonny. I would be bringing charges against him. I would force him to suffer as he forced you. And you, after all you have suffered, you choose to forgive."

She descended the final steps, and now, standing on the same level as the rest, she seemed almost ordinary. The ice goddess from the top of the stairs was just a thin girl trying hard not to weep.

He wanted desperately to protect her. Idiot, he thought. You have failed to protect her.

He held out his hand to his bride and she took it. Her skin was so cold. He gathered her in, pulling off his coat, wrapping her up. "Gordon," he ordered, "put your coat around Mrs. Stratton. They are freezing."

He could not know how relieved Devonny was when he jumped to the wrong conclusion and accidentally supplied an explanation for where she had been. They assumed Father was responsible. She would never correct them.

Armed with his hammer, standing in front of those who opposed him, Hugh-David did not look at all the way she remembered him. He looked handsome, and brave, and a little bit silly. She found herself smiling.

"How would you have cared for my mother?" she said.

"He didn't know," snapped a monstrously huge woman in a vast fur robe, who could only be Hugh-David's mother. "He was just stumbling around hoping things would work out."

How courageous of him to stand up to his bear of a mother. Devonny knew what it was like; she had a bear of a father. "I thank you, Winnie," said Devonny, who also knew what it was to stumble around hoping things would work out. "I thank you for your faith in me. I thank you for coming against my father's will, and against the law, to save my mother. I admit that I did not respect you, Winnie, but now I do. You have character, and strength of mind, and I will always think well of you."

"I was hoping you would not call me Winnie," he said.

"I think it fits quite well," she said. "I absolve you from any pledge. You may return to your country with honor, for you have treated me honorably, even in my absence, and in the face of a laughing public."

Instead of bowing gracefully and turning to leave, Hugh-David took both her hands. "Miss Stratton," he said humbly, "will you marry me after all?"

"What?" shrieked his mother. "You have narrowly escaped an alliance with these awful people! I forbid this!"

"What?" yelled Hiram Stratton. "You will get no dowry from me!"

"See?" shouted the Duchess. "There is no point to this without the settlement!"

Lord Winden knelt.

Devonny thought of loneliness and compromise and rescue. She thought of love and honor. She thought of the world she had nearly lost. She thought of the frail and desperate mother in the shadows, where already too much time had been spent.

Angry parents were shrieking. Winnie did not see or hear them, and neither did she.

"I have grown up a little," said Hugh-David. "I too would like to marry a person with character and strength, and that is you."

The yelling of parents receded into the distance. To be wanted for her strength was a beautiful thing. She would have liked to tell Tod. She felt a terrible pang. She would never be able to show anything off to Tod.

"There will be no mistresses," she told Hugh-David.

"No."

"There will be no gambling."

"No."

She thought of her travel through time; of her dear brother, whom she would never meet again, but whom Annie had lifted, somehow, into Egypt and archaeology. She said to Hugh-David, "When you travel to places like India, I will go along. You will never leave me behind."

"Yes."

She thought of Tod's designer water and his soccer team and his amazing mother and the great privilege it had been to share, so briefly, their world. "If I decide to start a business, you will not interfere."

"Start a business?" said Hugh-David, his jaw dropping.

"The children," said Devonny, "will have the names I choose." For the girls she would choose Annie and Harriett, and for the boys, Lockwood and Stratton.

"Wait," said Hugh-David. "Wait just a minute. I did not agree to that."

Devonny's stepmother and Devonny's mother exchanged happy smiles. "They sound married already, don't they?" said Florinda.

"I think they will get along very well," agreed Aurelia.

"Let's plan the wedding," said Florinda.

"No!" shouted Hugh-David's mother. "Not without a contract."

"Never!" shouted Hiram. "I have suffered enough! I am not paying for the privilege!"

"We have a contract," said Devonny. "It is signed. It is legal. Father has no choice. There is a dowry, Winnie, and it is the same one you thought you were getting. Father had the best lawyers, the tightest arrangements, and the firmest phrasing." She smiled, for she was truly happy. She had learned the most important thing, and it had nothing to do with one century or another. To help a stranger was what counted; to care for one another. And in both centuries, the people who mattered had done so. Including her husband-to-be.

"And this time," said Devonny Aurelia Victoria Stratton to her future husband, "I insist upon a new wedding gown."

# ABOUT THE AUTHOR

Caroline B. Cooney is the author of *The Face on the Milk Carton* (an IRA-CBC Children's Choice) and its companions, *Whatever Happened to Janie?* (an ALA Best Book for Young Adults) and *The Voice on the Radio; Driver's Ed; Among Friends;* and *Both Sides of Time* and *Out of Time,* companions to *Prisoner of Time.* She lives in Westbrook, Connecticut.